Frank grinned like an idiot and followed Laura to the right.

Janice had never seen Frank act so complacent before. It wasn't like him at all.

As soon as Frank and Laura left, she lowered her head. Trevor lowered his head at the same time.

"It's not going to work," they whispered in unison.

Any other time, Janice would have laughed. Today, nothing was funny. Not only had Laura and Frank booked the church, but over the next months, she was supposed to start in helping her friend make all the wedding arrangements. And that meant spending a lot of time with Trevor Halliday, a man she barely knew.

She struggled with the fact that this was really happening. Now, while she was expected to sit and talk to Trevor over coffee, Frank and Laura were off to buy the rings. For the wedding. The wedding that shouldn't happen.

GAIL SATTLER lives in Vancouver, BC (where you don't have to shovel rain) with her husband, three sons, two dogs, two lizards, and countless fish, many of whom have names. She writes inspirational romance because she loves happily-ever-afters and believes God has a place in that happy ending. Visit Gail's website at www.gailsattler.com.

HEARTSONG PRESENTS

Don't miss out on any of our super romances. Write to us at the following address for information on our newest releases and club membership.

Heartsong Presents Readers' Service
PO Box 721
Uhrichsville, OH 44683

Or visit us at www.heartsongpresents.com

The Wedding's On

Gail Sattler

Heartsong Presents

Dedicated to Lil Sattler,
my mother-in-law,
just because I love you.

A note from the author:
I love to hear from my readers! You may correspond with me by writing:

> **Gail Sattler**
> **Author Relations**
> **PO Box 719**
> **Uhrichsville, OH 44683**

ISBN 1-58660-524-0

THE WEDDING'S ON

All scripture quotations, unless otherwise indicated, are taken from the HOLY BIBLE, NEW INTERNATIONAL VERSION. NIV®. Copyright © 1973, 1978, 1984 by International Bible Society. Used by permission of Zondervan Publishing House. All rights reserved.

All of the characters and events in this book are fictitious. Any resemblance to actual persons, living or dead, or to actual events is purely coincidental.

Cover design by Randy Hamblin.

PRINTED IN THE U.S.A.

one

"Oh, Janice! I'm getting married!"

Janice Neufeld nearly dropped her coffee cup onto the kitchen floor. She watched Laura, her best friend, spin around, raise her hands above her head, then flop backward against the wall.

"Married?!" Janice sputtered. "To whom?"

Laura's eyelids fluttered shut, and she sighed. "Why, to Frank, of course."

Janice blinked and shook her head. "Frank? Frank Magnussen? How can that be? You two barely just met! How long have you known him? Two months?"

Laura lowered her arms and hugged herself, opened her eyes, then sighed again. Her dreamy expression almost made Janice want to throw up.

"I know it hasn't been long, but it's just so. . ." Laura sighed again. "So right!"

"I don't believe this," Janice muttered, shaking her head. Suddenly, she froze. If she thought she felt sick before, she really felt sick now at the thought of one reason why her friend would be rushing to get married. Even though it was wrong in God's sight, Christians were not immune to temptation. "You're, uh—not—you know."

Laura giggled. "No, silly. We're just in love. But he'll probably want to start a family pretty soon."

"Probably? You don't know? Just how much *do* you know about him?"

"Enough to know that we're going to be very happy together."

Janice fought to think rationally. She had known Frank longer than Laura had. Because of that, Janice knew him much

5

better—so much so that Janice didn't see how a relationship between Frank and Laura could possibly work. Knowing Frank as well as she did, Janice didn't know how Laura and Frank managed to stay in the same room without arguing. While it was said that opposites attract, Laura and Frank were one pair that were too opposite in things that really mattered.

However, it appeared Laura and Frank did have one thing in common. Apparently, they both wanted to get married.

Janice doubted that was enough to last the test of time.

She forced herself to keep a grip on her coffee cup, when what she really felt like doing was waving her hands in the air in utter frustration. "But you hardly know Frank. Do you know his likes and dislikes? His hobbies and interests? His future goals? Does he even like kids or even want kids at all—never mind right away? How does he feel about your rabbit? Not all guys like caged pets, you know."

Laura waved one hand in the air. "You're worrying for nothing. Just be happy for me."

Janice sucked in a deep breath. She never thought one word would be so hard to force out.

"Congratulations," she said.

She only wished she meant it.

ﾇﾓ

Trevor Halliday choked on his coffee. "Laura Merring? Are you nuts?"

Trevor's best friend raised his arms in the air, linked his fingers behind his head so his elbows stuck out to the sides, then flopped back against the doorframe. "Yeah." Frank sighed lazily. "Maybe I am. But I am serious. We're getting married."

Trevor wiped his mouth on his sleeve as he finished sputtering, then rested the coffee mug on the kitchen counter. "I thought you two just met not long ago."

Frank grinned. "We did. I can't explain it."

Trevor shook his head. "Yeah, well, neither can I. Does insanity run in your family? I didn't know you knew her that well."

Frank's grin turned so sappy that Trevor wanted to shake

some sense into him. "I know her well enough."

Trevor doubted that. He'd known Laura for a couple of years, which was about a year and ten months longer than Frank had known her. And knowing the two of them as he did, Trevor didn't see this as a match made in heaven. "I don't know about that. How much time have you really spent with her? I mean, quality time. She's never even been here, to our home, has she? How does she feel about Freddie?"

"Don't worry, Trev. She's cool. She won't mind Freddie."

Trevor had his doubts about that too. He wasn't too fond of Freddie, himself. He had a sneaking suspicion that Laura wouldn't be too fond of the nine-foot Burmese python either, especially on feeding day, as he knew Laura tended to be squeamish. "If you say so, Frank."

"I say so." Frank walked to the calendar hanging on the wall, paged through it, and circled a day in red.

Trevor peeked over his shoulder. "What are you doing?"

"Circling my wedding day, my friend. You gonna be my best man?"

Something in Trevor's stomach went to war with the coffee he'd just swallowed. "That's only four months away. You're only twenty-four years old. You don't have to rush. Unless. . ." A sick feeling settled in the pit of his stomach. His friend was a good Christian man who was supposed to be waiting for marriage, just as Trevor was.

Frank grinned. "Don't worry. It's not that. We booked the church today because we don't want the same thing to happen to us as it did to my sister. Remember the mess when she took too long to make arrangements when she got married?"

Trevor shook his head. "But you hardly know Laura! God wants us to love our wives, to treat them with respect, and be partners, sharing everything." He couldn't see Frank and Laura being partners in anything, least of all marriage.

"This wasn't the response I was expecting out of you. I thought you'd be happy to get the place to yourself."

Trevor swallowed hard. Instead of criticizing his friend's

judgment, as the future best man he knew what he should say. One word had never been so difficult.

"Congratulations," he choked out.

"Thanks." Frank smiled ear to ear. "Are you busy tomorrow night? I think maybe it would be a good time to get together and discuss stuff. Laura's friend Janice Neufeld is going to be her maid of honor. Do you remember her? Short little thing. Brown eyes, brown hair. Wears glasses."

He remembered Laura's friend. Laura was everything Janice was not. Laura was tall, blond, thin, and always in the center of the action. Janice, on the other hand, struck him as simply ordinary. "Yes, I've met her a few times."

"Great. I'm not sure what goes on behind the scenes in a wedding, but I know there'll be lots to do. You two should probably sit down and talk about stuff."

Frank stuck his hands in his pockets and sauntered into the living room, whistling the wedding march.

Trevor remained in the kitchen, his hands glued to his ceramic coffee mug. He couldn't let his friend set himself up for the heartache of an unhappy marriage. He didn't know what he was going to do, but he had to do something.

❧

Janice followed Laura, Frank, and Frank's friend, Trevor, into the mall. Once inside, they stopped a few feet beyond the entrance.

Frank pointed to the left. "If you guys don't mind, Laura and I are going to go to the sport shop."

Laura pointed to the right. "Don't you think we should go to the jewelry store first, Darling?"

"Oh, yeah. I guess. We'll meet you back at the food court in ten minutes."

Laura shook her head as she checked her watch. "Make that half an hour."

Frank grinned like an idiot and followed Laura to the right.

Janice had never seen Frank act so complacent before. It wasn't like him at all.

As soon as Frank and Laura left, she lowered her head. Trevor lowered his head at the same time.

"It's not going to work," they whispered in unison.

Any other time, Janice would have laughed. Today, nothing was funny. Not only had Laura and Frank booked the church, but over the next months, she was supposed to start helping her friend make all the wedding arrangements. And that meant spending a lot of time with Trevor Halliday, a man she barely knew.

She struggled with the fact that this was really happening. Now, while she was expected to sit and talk to Trevor over coffee, Frank and Laura were off to buy the rings. For the wedding. The wedding that shouldn't happen.

Even though it was Saturday, the food court wasn't crowded, allowing Janice and Trevor to select a relatively private table once they purchased a cup of coffee apiece.

Trevor leaned back in the chair and folded his arms across his chest. "If you're going to be Laura's maid of honor, I guess that means you know her pretty well. Is she really serious?"

Janice arched one eyebrow. "I was going to ask you the same thing about Frank."

They both stared at each other until Trevor cleared his throat. He leaned forward, lowered his head, and studied his coffee cup very intently as he spoke. "This probably isn't going to sound too great, but I'm really concerned that Frank is making a mistake." He raised his head but didn't release the plastic cup. "Not that I have anything against Laura. I like Laura. I just think they should take more time to get to know each other." He didn't break eye contact as he picked up the cup and sipped the hot coffee, then slowly lowered it to the tabletop.

"In other words, you think that if they got to know each other better, they'd see that getting married is a dumb idea."

Trevor's ears turned red, and he stared down into his coffee cup. "I wouldn't have put it quite so succinctly, but yes, that's exactly what I meant."

Janice froze, then stared down into her own coffee cup. "I

didn't mean that quite as badly as it sounded, but I'm glad you agree. The trouble is, I don't know what to do about it. I can't sit back and let Laura make what could possibly be the biggest mistake of her life." Janice felt the heat rising in her cheeks as she lifted her face to look back at Trevor, who was now looking up at her too. "Don't get me wrong. I like Frank. I really do. But knowing Laura, I don't know how those two even stay in the same room together. I can't imagine them being married. I really don't know what to do. All I know is that I have to do something."

"Same here. I don't want to see Frank make a mistake about something so important either."

Janice looked more closely at Trevor. Even though he didn't attend the same church as she and Laura, she knew he did attend regularly at his own church, with Frank. From past times she'd met him, she considered his faith to be solid and believed he lived his life according to God's direction to the best of his ability. Knowing that he felt the same way about their friends' upcoming marriage gave her more conviction that she was right. Or, if not right, at least she had just cause for concern.

Not wanting to get caught talking about their friends, Janice glanced over her shoulder to make sure Frank and Laura weren't on their way back yet. They weren't, but she lowered her voice to a whisper anyway. "So, what do you think we should do?"

Trevor also lowered his voice. "I don't know. I thought about it all night, ever since I found out, and I can't think of anything. Normally, I'd be inclined to let time take its course, but I don't know if that's such a good idea in this case."

She nodded, then adjusted her glasses when they slipped down her nose. "I know what you mean. The wedding is four months away. That gives us some amount of leeway but not a lot. Maybe we should just watch them closely for a month and see how it goes. Although I hate to start making arrangements and putting down deposits and down payments when the outcome is still uncertain."

"I know what you mean. Do you have any idea how much it costs to rent a tux?"

Janice grinned wryly. "Do you have any idea how much it costs to have a bridesmaid dress made? It's even worse spending all that money and knowing you're only going to wear it once. Or in this case, hopefully never."

"I never thought of it that way. Why don't women just rent the dresses?"

At his question, Trevor grinned. Janice's breath caught. She'd been with Trevor in a group many times before today but never realized how attractive he was when he smiled. He wasn't old enough to have laugh lines, but she could see little crinkles starting to develop at the corners of his eyes, something she'd always found attractive in men.

Really looking at him for possibly the first time, she reevaluated him. He wasn't exactly movie-star handsome, but despite his big nose, he wasn't bad-looking. That she'd never been attracted to the blond-haired, blue-eyed types before probably explained why she'd never taken notice of him. Frank was the one who was tall, dark, and handsome, although he wasn't quite as tall as Trevor by about an inch. Now that she did decide to pay attention to Trevor, he wasn't hard on the eyes at all.

Janice shook her head. She wasn't there to ogle Frank's friend. Also, just because he was good-looking didn't mean she had to like him or pretend that she wanted to become friends with him. She was only there to make sure her own friend wasn't heading into the biggest disaster of her life.

She glanced over her shoulder once again. "Never mind about the clothes. We have to think of something before they get back."

They both sat in silence, staring at each other, thinking.

An idea popped into Janice's head. She opened her mouth to speak, but before she could get a word out, a familiar voice sounded behind her.

"Hey! Janice! Look what Frank gave me!"

Her mouth snapped shut. Automatically, Janice looked down to Laura's hand. Her ring finger was still bare.

Janice tipped her head up to meet her friend's eyes, but a sparkle around Laura's neck caught her attention.

"A diamond necklace! It's beautiful!" She jumped to her feet to examine it. If Frank could buy an engagement ring at the same time as such an expensive trinket, he had more money than she realized.

Trevor stood as well, but he didn't appear to be as interested in the necklace as Janice. "Why did you buy a necklace? I thought you two were going to buy an engagement ring."

Laura slipped her arm around Frank's waist. "We did. We bought both. And wedding rings too. We have to wait a couple of days for the rings to be sized. But look what Frank got me to make up for it."

Dollar signs flashed before Janice's eyes. "Don't you think that's a rather large expenditure just before a wedding?"

Frank shrugged his shoulders. "That's okay. I charged it. I don't have to pay for it for a long time."

"You. . ." Laura's voice trailed off, and her eyes widened. "You didn't tell me that. I hope you intend to pay for all this before the wedding."

"I don't know. I'll have to see how much overtime I get."

"Overtime?"

"Yeah. You know I have to work a lot of overtime. Trev loves it. He gets first dibs on the television."

"But. . . ," Laura sputtered.

Before she could say another word, Frank turned to her. With his index finger, he lifted the center of the diamond necklace, then smiled. Laura's mouth closed, and she tipped her head up to gaze back at Frank with stars in her eyes.

Janice wanted to throw up. She leaned toward Trevor. "Just how long does Frank work each day? I don't think Laura wants to get married so she can stay home alone and watch television. She doesn't even watch that much television."

Trevor lowered his head and whispered back. "He's teasing. He doesn't work late that often. It's just that when he does, it's long hours. Neither of us watches much television since

most of the shows are junk. We recently talked about cancel-
ing the cable service."

Janice's eyes widened. "Really? Us too."

"Hey, you two!" Laura said as she tapped her foot on the
hard floor. The noise echoed down the mall. "Quit whisper-
ing. I'm hungry."

Frank rubbed his stomach with one hand. "Yeah. Who
wants pizza?"

Laura rested her hand inside the crook of Frank's elbow.
"Mushroom and pepperoni? At Alberto's?"

Frank smiled. "My favorite."

Janice whispered to Trevor out of the corner of her mouth.
"At least there's something they agree on. Maybe there is
hope, after all."

He mumbled something she couldn't hear, which was probably just as well.

Together, the four exited the mall to their cars.

Janice had come to the mall with Laura in Laura's car, and
Trevor had arrived with Frank in Frank's car. Somehow, instead
of being with her friend, Janice now found herself traveling
with Trevor, and Frank had taken her place in Laura's car.

She didn't want to ride with Trevor. She needed to talk
to Laura.

They had to discuss the necklace. Issues about money com-
monly affected the success or failure of a marriage. Laura was
best described as "thrifty." Frank's impulsive and extravagant
gift came at a time when the money could have been spent
more wisely, especially when he didn't really have the money
in the first place. If this was an indication of Frank's spending
habits, already things didn't bode well for a good start to their
impending marriage. What she didn't understand was that
Laura seemed genuinely pleased Frank had bought the necklace. Knowing Laura's eagle eye for price tags, Janice had no
doubt that Laura knew the cost before Frank bought it.

Trevor's voice broke into her thoughts. "What if we're
wrong? What if they're more suited to each other than we

think? Frank is my best friend. I don't want to ruin the relationship if it is the right thing. But if it's not, I can't stand by and let him make a big mistake."

Janice stared out the window of the moving vehicle, unable to look at him as she spoke. "I'm just as confused by this whole thing as you are."

"Every time I think one way, they do something to confuse me. The bottom line is that they obviously like each other. But I'm not sure if liking is enough of a basis for marriage. They've known each other such a short amount of time."

Janice turned to him and nodded. "I know exactly what you mean. I've known you longer than Laura has known Frank. And I'm not about to marry you." Janice slapped her hands over her mouth. "Oops! I didn't mean that the way it sounded."

"That's okay. I don't want to marry you either."

Janice felt her mouth drop open as she turned and stared at him. He didn't turn his head. Instead, he paid more attention to the road than he had the entire trip so far. He clenched his teeth on his lower lip, and Janice could see the corners of his mouth quivering.

She steadied her glasses on her nose with her index finger. "You are sooooo not funny," she muttered, then cleared her throat. "What I meant was, Laura isn't flaky or anything. She's had only two serious boyfriends since high school. She's not the type to fall in and out of love easily. The relationship with the one guy she claimed she had fallen in love with didn't last, but while it was on, she never stopped talking about him. What makes this so strange is that I never heard any declarations of being in love with Frank. I didn't even know she had been seriously dating anyone. When she told me she was getting married, I didn't know who the lucky man was."

All traces of humor instantly left Trevor's face. He emitted a strangled, choking sound, quickly glanced behind them, pulled the car to the side of the road, and stopped abruptly.

"The same happened with Frank. I didn't know he and Laura were dating either. The next thing I know, he's circling a wedding date on the calendar."

A throbbing sensation started above Janice's left eye, which usually meant the beginning of a migraine. With all the tension of the day, she shouldn't have been surprised. First, she had been nearly overwhelmed with guilt at her wish to stop Laura and Frank from getting married, at least right away. Then, she let herself hope against hope that Laura and Frank really could be happy together, even though she didn't see how. Now, an impending sense of doom washed over her as she pictured that in the not-too-distant future, she would be helping Laura deal with the pain of divorce.

While divorce was frowned on in the church, no one could deny that it happened—and to good people. Despite the apparent ease of divorce in today's society, she had witnessed its effects on people she knew, both Christians and non-Christians alike. Divorce was painful and difficult, leaving much devastation in its wake.

When the day came for her to get married, Janice vowed she would be obedient to follow God's direction. She fully intended for her own marriage to last forever. Following God's guidelines meant that when she met her Mr. Right and agreed to marry him, there could be no doubt that she was making the right decision. In order to be prepared, she planned to know the man who would be her husband far better than Laura knew Frank. She also would need to be assured in concrete ways that they shared common interests and goals. She would have to know beyond a shadow of doubt that their compatibility would withstand the test of time.

Janice lowered her voice, although she didn't know why. It was just the two of them in the car. Slowly, she massaged the tender spot above her left eyebrow with her fingers. "We've got to show them how unsuited they are for each other. I have an idea." She stopped and looked Trevor straight in the eyes. She could see him stiffen with the intensity of her gaze.

She cleared her throat. "But I'm going to need your help—and lots of it."

two

Suddenly, the air in the car became unreasonably stuffy. Trevor turned off the motor and rolled the window down. Without breaking eye contact with Janice, he moved his face closer to the window and inhaled a deep breath of the cool evening air to clear his head.

He didn't know what he'd been thinking, but it hadn't been to make plots and plans behind Frank's back. However, he didn't know how he had thought the end result would have been anything different. Realistically, he knew that agreeing about Frank and Laura's unsuitability as mates with Laura's friend wouldn't make the problem go away, nor would merely discussing the problem solve it. He just hadn't thought about it to the logical conclusion, which was to be prepared to actively do something about it.

His vision blurred, not really seeing Janice even though he was looking straight at her.

A voice in his head echoed that he had no business interfering with Frank's love life. Worse than interfering, he was now involving himself in making a secret scheme that would no doubt hurt his best friend.

Another little voice battled the first little voice. What kind of friend was he if all he did was complain to Janice, agree that his friend was making a mistake, and then watch it happen? The answer was: a rotten friend. It was his duty and responsibility to guide Frank if he saw Frank doing something wrong.

Not that getting married was wrong—the issue was Frank's judgment in his choice of Laura as the perfect wife. Not that there was anything wrong with Laura. Trevor just didn't see her as a good match for Frank.

Trevor exhaled deeply and refocused on Janice. The second she saw she had his attention, she started listing numerous reasons she thought Frank and Laura weren't suited to each other. As if he needed convincing.

Nothing of what she outlined came as a surprise. Still, the more she said, the heavier the weight of guilt settled on his shoulders at what he had to do. Over and over, he reminded himself that both he and Janice were only trying to do what was best for their friends in the long run.

A verse from Matthew ran through his head, the one about every matter being established by the testimony of two or three witnesses. The more he listened to Janice, the more he became convinced that they were justified in their concern—justified enough to do something about it.

In the end, if Frank and Laura were suited to each other, then what Trevor and Janice were about to do would strengthen the relationship and thereby help to cement the basis for a strong marriage. If what they were about to do broke up the relationship before the wedding, then it was right that the wedding should never take place. Either way, Janice's concerns strengthened his growing convictions that they were doing the right thing after all. What they were doing, they were doing out of love for their Christian brother and sister, who also happened to be their best friends.

Janice cleared her throat. "Well? What do you think? Do you think that's a good idea?"

All Trevor could do was blink. Basically, her plan was for him to make an extensive list of Frank's personality traits, good and bad, as well as Frank's likes and dislikes. At the same time, Janice would make a similar list for Laura. Then, they would trade lists. Trevor was to sit with Frank and ask Frank his needs and wants of the woman who would be his wife, as well as what Frank thought he would bring into the relationship that Laura would want. Trevor would refer to Janice's list about Laura to either prove or disprove whether Frank and Laura were a match. At the same time, Janice would do the same with

Laura and the list Trevor made about Frank.

He cleared his throat. "I know we don't know each other very well, and I hope you'll take this in the spirit in which it was meant. I think it's a lousy idea."

She crossed her arms and leaned back in her seat. "Oh? Why?"

"You're on the right track, but I don't think it's going to work. I don't ever question Frank about women he's dating, and especially not if the relationship is serious. Not that there have been many, you understand. I don't think asking him to provide a list of characteristics he would like in the woman he wants to marry is going to do anything except make him mad. I can tell you that if I suddenly start spouting negative answers to questions about Laura in comparison to what he thinks he should be hearing, he won't believe me. At least not when I read the answers off a list that *you* wrote. He has to learn that stuff for himself, right from Laura."

She leaned closer. Even in the dark, he could see her eyes widen behind her glasses. "But don't you see?" she asked. "There isn't time for that. I don't know why they can't see those things about each other, so we have to show them."

He shook his head. "I'm no psych major. I can't analyze and mix and match personality traits from a list. Pointing out to the two of them that Frank wants to live in an apartment close to downtown where the action is, and Laura's dream is having acreage on the outskirts of town in order to be closer to the cows doesn't mean they're going to agree that they wouldn't make good marriage partners. I don't know enough about stuff like that to know what things make opposites attract and what things drive a person nuts about another person."

"But we've got to get them to see this realistically. To talk about it. Right now, Laura can't see past the stars in her eyes."

Trevor dragged his palm down his face. "Right. Get them to talk about it. And how do you suppose we're going to bring this up in conversation?" Trevor cleared his throat and deepened his voice while he waved one hand in the air. "Hey,

Frank, old buddy. Janice and I made a list of the things Laura wants in a husband. And guess what? You don't match up with a single one." He let the silence hang.

Janice made some kind of strange snort, which Trevor thought quite unfeminine. "And what's wrong with that?" she grumbled.

Trevor ran his fingers through his hair. "I can't believe you're being so pragmatic about this. You're completely missing the point here. Didn't you see the way he was looking at her? They think they're in love, and maybe they are! And you're adding up lists of personality traits in a tidy package. Like the mathematics of the negatives will outweigh the positives. It doesn't work that way. You're a woman, for crying out loud! Think *romancey* stuff!"

"You're shouting."

Trevor bowed his head slightly and pinched the bridge of his nose. "Sorry," he mumbled.

She crossed her arms over her chest. "So, you have a better idea, I suppose?"

Trevor started the engine. "No, I don't. But I do know one thing. If we don't get to the restaurant soon, they're going to think we were in an accident and call 911. We'll have to think of something else later."

They made the rest of the trip in silence.

He'd barely stopped the car before they pushed the doors open and ran across the parking lot. They skidded to a halt at the entrance, stiffened their backs, and tried to appear carefree as they entered the dining area.

Frank studied his watch and raised his eyebrows as Trevor and Janice lowered themselves into the waiting chairs. "We were getting worried that you'd had an accident or something. Is everything okay?"

Trevor nodded. "Everything is fine. We just stopped to talk for a couple of minutes."

"Stopped to talk?" Frank glanced back and forth between Trevor and Janice, then smiled. "Oh. To talk. That's cool."

Without clarifying what he meant or dwelling further on it, Frank turned to Janice. "It looks like you'll be seeing me at your church tomorrow. I've decided to make Laura's church my home, since we have to decide between the two. It wouldn't be right for us to go to different churches. Besides, we booked the ceremony at your church." He turned back to Trevor. "So it looks like you'll be going alone tomorrow morning, old man."

The gears started whirring in Trevor's head. He didn't know why it took so long, but it suddenly dawned on him that Frank didn't believe that he and Janice had stopped to simply talk. With that in mind, he formulated a plan of his own.

A plan that would work.

Now if he could just figure out a way to let Janice know what he was doing without Frank and Laura catching on. . .

❧

Janice stared at Frank, trying to think of what this new development would mean. She and Laura always went to church together. They usually sat together, but not always. Still, no matter where they sat, since they always arrived in the same car, one never made plans without the other. Now, since Laura had invited Frank, she didn't know if she would be included or not. Nor did she know how to ask if she would be going alone to church or if she would be the odd man out and make it a threesome. Neither held much appeal.

She tried to think of a way to ask the question without sounding stupid when Trevor spoke up beside her.

He smiled politely at Frank. "I won't be going alone. I'm going to be joining Janice tomorrow morning, so it looks like we can still drive together after all, at least to Janice and Laura's."

Janice turned to stare at Trevor.

Before she had a chance to ask him what he was talking about, he turned his head and reached toward her. Gently, he rested his palm on her forearm. At his touch, her words stalled in her brain. All she could do was stare at his hand, his touch warming her.

Trevor's voice came out in a low rumble. Despite his hushed tones, she knew Laura would still be able to hear him. "I know you said you wanted it to be just the two of us, but would you mind if we sat with Frank and Laura? Maybe they can join us for lunch afterward?"

"But. . . ," she sputtered, letting her voice trail off. "I never. . ."

Something tapped her sharply at the ankle. To prevent herself from saying anything stupid, she took a long sip of her coffee to give herself some time to figure out what was going on.

Trevor continued. "If you want, we can still go alone. But maybe it would be fun—you know, like a double date, for lunch after church."

Janice nearly choked on her coffee, something she noticed had been happening a lot over the last couple of days. To imply there would be a change to make it a *double date* meant that a single date had been planned, and it had not.

"Janice!" Laura chimed. Janice turned her head to face Laura, whose fingers were firmly intertwined with Frank's atop the table. "I didn't know you and Trevor were seeing each other. How exciting!"

Janice blinked repeatedly. The only reason she'd seen Trevor at all was because of Laura. She certainly would never have chosen to see him on her own.

She turned back to Trevor, who had quit touching her arm. He was now nonchalantly leaning back in his chair, his arms crossed over his chest. He was also grinning like an idiot. Beneath the table, Trevor's foot kept nudging her ankle.

Janice sucked in a deep breath. "It kind of caught me off guard too," she grumbled.

The rest of their time together passed quickly and smoothly. Still, even though Frank and Laura didn't argue or disagree about anything verbally, Janice could see that they were worlds apart on many of their discussion topics. More than ever, she knew she had to do something to get Laura to see their differences.

Not for the first time, the guilt at what she wanted to do

assailed her. All she wanted was for her friend to be happy. If that meant for Laura to marry Frank, then that was well and good. However, the more time she spent with Laura and Frank as a couple, the less she could foresee them being happy together on a day-to-day basis.

The more she thought about what Trevor had said in the car, the more she could see he was right. Pointing out to Laura that Frank was not the man of her dreams would not work. The only way for Laura to change her mind was through direct interaction with Frank to discover their differences for herself.

As partners, she and Trevor could gently point out areas of compatibility or incompatibility while Frank and Laura were together. Maybe if they did it right, Frank and Laura might not realize their involvement. Done carefully and correctly, Frank and Laura might even think that they came to the realization that they really weren't suited for each other by themselves.

Again, Trevor was right, in theory. Certainly, she and Trevor would have to spend time with Frank and Laura as a couple in order to do this. However, trying to disguise it as a double date was going about it in the wrong way. If it weren't for her friend, she wouldn't be with Trevor at all. She most certainly wouldn't be dating him. She didn't know him very well, but she knew him well enough to know that there was nothing about him that she specifically liked and much about him that she didn't like.

First of all, he was too pushy and impatient. Janice always preferred a man who was gentle and soft-spoken. The first time they had ever been alone together he had shouted at her. She hated being yelled at, especially when all she had done was express her opinion and subsequent thoughts on a plan of action.

She also wasn't too fond of his thrown-together strategy to double-date in order to get closer to their friends without discussing it with her first. Janice thought her idea made much more sense because at least she had a specific plan. Despite the fact that it wouldn't work, it was still a well-thought-out plan. He'd blurted his plan out and put it into action before he'd logically reasoned it out. Janice knew without doubt that spending Sunday afternoon together under the guise of a double date wouldn't solve the problem.

However, what was done was done. She had no alternative but to follow through with Trevor's plan—already set in motion. For now, it was the best they could do in their quest to show Frank and Laura their misconceptions about each other.

They didn't have time to lose. A wedding date of four months down the road was now circled on the calendar in her kitchen.

Therefore, she had no alternative but to pretend to be dating Trevor Halliday.

Janice steeled her nerve and smiled at Trevor, who was smiling at her, making her realize she had missed most of the conversation and had no idea what he'd just said.

"Great," Trevor murmured. "I can hardly wait until Tuesday, then, when I can see that new dress. You're so pretty in blue."

She forced herself to keep smiling. She seldom wore dresses, even to church. She only owned two dresses, and neither of them was blue. The only blue things she owned were blue jeans. Instead of showing everyone that she hadn't been paying attention, she would ask Trevor later what they had allegedly scheduled for Tuesday. She would also tell him whatever it was she'd agreed to, she had no intention of wearing a dress.

When the pizzas came, they paused to pray over their meal. Conversation continued on neutral and insignificant topics, giving Janice a chance to study the man whom she was supposed to be dating. On the bright side, Janice reminded herself that dating was the way to get to know someone better. Since she was supposed to be dating Trevor, she could show Laura how the process of getting to know a man was supposed to be done. Not that she intended to get to know Trevor that well. She only had to know him well enough to accomplish their mutual purpose.

By the time they left the restaurant, she couldn't say she knew Trevor any better than when they went in, despite the change in their relationship status. Thinking back, she'd dated the one man she'd ever come close to being serious about for nearly a year before she got to know him reasonably well. And over that year, she'd never considered marrying him.

The four of them walked together into the parking lot. Janice doubted she would get the chance to talk to Trevor privately because this time, instead of getting into Trevor's car, she was destined to be Laura's passenger since they were all going home.

Once they reached the cars, she knew without a doubt that no matter how quietly she spoke, Frank and Laura would hear every word she said. She needed to ask Trevor a few things about himself in order to make it look like she really was dating him. As it was now, she could barely recall the color of his eyes.

Laura and Frank stepped to the side, but not out of hearing range.

Laura's voice dropped to a husky whisper. "Good night, Frank," she purred, shuffling closer to him. Frank lowered his head and gave Laura a chaste, but long, kiss.

Janice squirmed. If she was officially dating Trevor, she wondered if she was supposed to kiss him good night too. She wished she knew how long they were supposed to have been dating so far. And even if she had been allegedly dating him for awhile, she still wouldn't have kissed him in the middle of a parking lot.

Trevor grinned and stepped closer. Janice's stomach dropped to somewhere below her shoes. She really didn't want to kiss him. She barely knew him. What little of him she did know, she wasn't sure she liked, especially in light of his ridiculous masquerade.

Suddenly, she was toe-to-toe with him. He lowered his head. Janice gritted her teeth. She was well practiced in the art of self-defense, and she wasn't afraid to use it. If Trevor tried anything funny, she considered decking him, regardless of what Laura and Frank would think.

His lips brushed her hair at her temple, but instead of kissing her cheek, his palms rested on her shoulders. He whispered in her ear, "We have to talk."

Janice tipped her chin up, not to kiss his cheek but to whisper closer to his ear. In doing so, she made a mental note to remember that his eyes were blue. "You've got that right, buddy boy."

"Loosen up," he continued to whisper. "I should probably look like I'm kissing you, but you're so stiff it looks like you're ready to run the fifty-yard dash."

Running wasn't exactly what she had in mind, but it was probably better than the violence currently formulating in her head. "Where did you get this harebrained idea that we should let them think we're dating?" she hissed between her teeth.

"It came to me in a stroke of genius," he whispered back.

Janice wondered about his IQ level.

He continued to whisper. "I should phone you when I get home, but I don't want Frank to overhear. I'll think of something later."

Before she realized it, he'd backed up. However, he didn't release her shoulders. One finger gently brushed her lower cheek.

She narrowed her eyes and glared up at him. He removed his hands a split second before she would have smacked them off.

"Good night, Janice," he said softly, but loudly enough for Laura and Frank to hear. "I can hardly wait for tomorrow morning."

For the first time in her life, Janice didn't want to go to church.

If she didn't feel guilty enough for what she was trying to do, now more guilt piled on her head.

Trevor started to step away but stopped when they saw Frank and Laura talking in hushed tones, not separating.

He shuffled closer again, but fortunately, not as close as before.

"Sorry about earlier, but the idea just kind of hit me," he said softly. He quickly glanced at Frank and Laura, then turned back to Janice. "If they think we're dating, then we'll be able to be with them most of the time. You know, to keep tabs on them and stuff. But this won't work unless you're a little more convincing. You should act at least a little bit romantic if we're supposedly seeing each other."

Janice nearly choked. She didn't want to think of acting "romantic" toward Trevor when she didn't know him beyond the realm of a casual acquaintance. She knew her best friend's fiancé better than she knew her alleged boyfriend. However, since she didn't figure she had much time before Frank and Laura were finished talking, she focused on their primary concern. "Why are you doing this? We're never going to fool anyone."

"Don't worry about it. You saw them today—they couldn't agree on a single thing. I'm sure they're on the verge of seeing this isn't meant to be. We won't have to pretend we like each other for very long."

As Trevor backed up, his words echoed in her head. *Pretend we like each other.* Never in her wildest dreams or worst nightmares would she have foreseen the magnitude of what she had agreed to do.

Frank and Laura separated, and the two men quickly slipped into Frank's car.

Janice stood in one spot, her feet refusing to move. She pressed the fingertips of both hands to her throbbing temples. If she was lucky, maybe her headache would develop into a full migraine, then she would have a legitimate excuse for missing church and their scheduled "double date."

"Come on, Janice," Laura said as she opened the car door. "It's late, and we have to get up early in the morning."

three

As he stood with Frank on Janice and Laura's doorstep, Trevor strained to hear what Janice was trying to tell him.

He couldn't hear her over Laura's giggling.

Janice stepped away from Frank and Laura, so he stepped closer to Janice.

"What in the world are you wearing?" she ground out between her teeth in a stage whisper.

"Is this a trick question?" he asked as he raised one hand to the knot of his tie. As he did, he studied Janice, who was wearing fashionably snug jeans and a fluffy pink sweater. He looked further down. Instead of dress shoes, she wore sneakers.

Trevor cleared his throat. "Aren't we going to church?"

"Of course we're going to church. But it's a regular Sunday service. Not a funeral. You'd better come in. If you don't take off that suit jacket, everyone's going to stare at us."

A very bad premonition washed over him. He'd automatically chosen what he would have worn to his own church, which was his best monochrome pants and shirt ensemble with a matching sport coat and a plain tie. He'd grown up in a traditional church where all the men wore suits—or a reasonable facsimile. What he wore today was quite appropriate for a warm spring Sunday service.

It appeared her church was more laid-back than his.

Again, he looked down to her sneakers. He could almost see wearing jeans to a service if they were new and of a reasonably good quality brand name, but hers were neither. In addition to the condition of her jeans, he thought the sneakers were a bit much, no matter how relaxed the setting. "Are you seriously going to church like that? Or were you out in the park for a walk first?"

She laughed, probably thinking he was joking. "Of course not. I was right here, waiting for you."

Trevor checked his watch. "I guess we'd better get going."

As he turned, Janice grabbed him by the arm and pulled him inside. She held out her hand. "Wait. I'm being serious. You can't go like that to church."

"But. . ." He let his voice trail off at her stone-faced expression.

"No one ever wears a suit to Sunday service. You're going to look silly."

He opened his mouth to tell her that he was quite appropriately dressed for a Sunday service, but before he could form an argument, he stopped himself. He didn't know Janice well, but he did know from previous occasions that once Janice set her mind to something, she stuck to it like a dog with an old bone.

He sighed as he shrugged off the jacket and handed it to her, telling himself that he was doing this for Frank, not for Janice.

She slung the jacket over one arm and held out her free hand. "Come on, Trevor. Lose the tie."

Automatically, he rested his palm in the center of his chest, over his tie. "No. I haven't been to church without a tie since I was a kid. I can't go to church without a tie." The only times he didn't wear a tie to church was once a year at the church picnic, when they had the service in the park. Even then, it felt funny.

"Quit fooling around. We don't have time for this."

He stiffened his back and shook his head. "I'm not fooling around. This has gone far enough. It's not proper to go to church without a tie."

She sighed loudly and tilted her head toward their friends. "Look. Frank is taking off his jacket and the tie too. Can't you just do the same, nicely?"

Trevor gritted his teeth and slipped off the tie, even though it went completely against his grain. Knowing Frank really didn't know much about Laura, he should have guessed that Frank wouldn't have known anything about her church either, even though he should have. After all, this was supposedly the church Frank had chosen to get married in and attend after the wedding.

The four of them went together in Frank's car, leaving Trevor to share the backseat with Janice. Conversation was stilted, and Janice spent most of the trip seated as close to the door as her seat belt would allow. Trevor chose not to comment. If she chose to be in a snit because he didn't agree with her dress code, that was up to her. He wasn't going to ruin his time of worship by arriving at church in a foul mood.

They soon arrived at a massive parking lot adjoining a large multifaceted brick building. The main entrance consisted only of plain double doors, which were at the base of what was probably the modern version of a bell tower. However, instead of a hollow space and a bell at the peak, a huge white cross graced the top. The building itself was a three-story structure graced with tall, rectangular, starkly plain glass windows. A large flat section extended to the back, which Trevor guessed would contain the classrooms.

As they walked in, Trevor could barely believe the size of the place, which somehow seemed even larger from the inside. Music drifted from the sanctuary—not hymns, but a contemporary chorus played by a whole band.

"How many people attend here?" he asked, leaning down so hopefully Janice was the only one who heard his question. His own church had a regular attendance of approximately three hundred people. He liked being a member of a congregation where he could know everyone, by face if not by name.

"I don't know. I suppose about twelve hundred people. There are two services Sunday morning, plus one in the evening. In the summertime they have a Saturday night service too. And on Friday, they always have youth and young adult functions. Lots of times I come here Friday night to play volleyball. There's a gymnasium down the hall."

It shouldn't have surprised him that there was another huge room he hadn't accounted for.

Just as Janice had said, everyone he could see was dressed casually. With the exception of a few of the older men present, most of those in attendance were under thirty years of age and wore jeans and a casual top. He did appear to be on the verge of overdressed. He would never admit it to Janice, but now he was grateful she'd made him take off his tie.

He continued to study the people milling about the foyer.

"Look," he whispered as he leaned down to Janice. "There's a guy in a tie." He jerked his thumb over his shoulder to direct her attention to the right person, as if she could miss him. He was the only one in the place wearing a tie, even if he wasn't wearing a jacket.

Janice poked Trevor in the stomach, making him bring both hands down to protect himself.

"Don't do that! He's the only one here who ever wears a tie, but he can do whatever he wants. He's my boss, Ken Quinlan. The woman with him is his wife, Molly. She's the one who led me to the Lord two years ago."

"Really? That's amazing. There's an older man who goes to my church named Walter Quinlan. I know that Walter never had kids, but I wonder if they're related? It's not a common name. Can you introduce me?"

Janice shook her head. "I can answer that. Walter is his uncle, and he used to be my boss. He still owns the company, but Ken started running it when Walter took an early retirement. Maybe I'll introduce you later. We're supposed to be with Frank and Laura, not socializing."

He followed her into the sanctuary. Unlike the ornate wooden benches in his church, the seating consisted of padded stacking chairs. Like the outside, the sanctuary was also void of any decoration except for a single cross at the front. Even the wooden podium was rather plain.

A few people in the front rows appeared to be praying and readying themselves to worship. Other than that, most people talked freely in the sanctuary.

Still, despite the lack of formality, the place held a certain appeal. Since it wasn't in the surroundings, Trevor figured the charm of Janice's church had to be in the spirit of the people present—all believers obviously happy to be in God's house on a Sunday morning.

His attention wandered to the speakers mounted near the ceiling at the front, which piqued his curiosity about the band's sound system. At the same time as he checked the place out, he reminded himself that this was the church Frank was getting married in. As much as the place was growing on him, it still made him wonder how Frank could have agreed to such a thing without seeing and experiencing the congregation first. This church was very different from theirs.

He felt a tug on his sleeve. "Come on. There they are. We'd better sit down now if we want to get seats beside them. This place fills up fast. The service starts in five minutes."

They took their places, and as Janice predicted, the service started exactly on time at ten o'clock.

To his surprise, he enjoyed the worship time, unexpectedly being able to forget about the crowd around him as he praised God in song. Still, he didn't lift his hands like most of the people around him, including Janice. He listened politely to the testimony of a teenaged girl who had recently come to the Lord through the church's extremely active youth group. In addition to being moved by her testimony, he greatly admired the girl for being able to speak so freely in front of a large group, something he knew he wouldn't be able to do.

The pastor was a dynamic speaker, moving the place up another notch on Trevor's scale. During the pastor's message, a number of people boldly called out "amen." One man called out a few comments that made many in the congregation laugh. Even the pastor laughed. For such a large place, Trevor was amazed that it could be so friendly.

At the close of the service, he didn't want to admit it, but he kind of liked the place. Still, he knew he would never consider attending on a regular basis. As nice as it was for a change, the informal atmosphere wasn't his style for a house of worship.

This time, he and Janice stuck close to Frank and Laura as they mingled with the people milling about. He recognized a few of Laura and Janice's friends from having met them before. Janice introduced him to everyone as they chatted for a few minutes and carried on the conversation, just in case he didn't remember their names, which he appreciated.

They were almost on their way out of the building when another couple joined them. Laura introduced them as Rick and Sarah, who were brother and sister.

Sarah and Rick remained close together, chatting with Janice in such a way that seemed to deliberately omit everyone else from the conversation. As the only relative stranger in the crowd, Trevor stood back to watch.

Trevor noted with amusement that much of Sarah's conversation centered on her brother and all his finer attributes. Rick had very little to say while his sister dribbled on and on, mentioning Rick at every opportunity, slipping little plugs into the conversation about what she considered Rick's best qualities.

Before long, Sarah began prompting Janice to say something. When Janice finally started adding more into the conversation, Sarah poked Rick in the back, much to Rick's annoyance, forcing him to step forward and participate more as well. At that point, Sarah shuffled slightly back, starting to edge out of the little group, leaving Rick talking solely to Janice.

Any other time, Trevor would have found such lack of subtlety in matchmaking hilarious. This time it wasn't funny.

Glancing out the corner of his eye, Trevor noticed Frank looking back and forth between himself and Rick as Rick's actions and conversation began to cross the line from small talk into serious flirtation. Laura stared unwavering at Janice. Neither of them made any attempt to break into the conversation.

Janice giggled at something Rick said.

Trevor gritted his teeth. Without warning, he stepped forward, placing himself directly between Rick and Janice, purposely standing much too close to Rick, invading Rick's personal space. He made a point to take advantage of his height, noticeably tipping his head to look down at Rick, who was only about average height. Rick quickly backed up a step, and his voice trailed off as he finished his sentence.

Trevor gave a lopsided grin and quirked one eyebrow. He sidestepped until he was side by side with Janice, then slipped one arm around her waist. "Sorry to interrupt, Rick, but we were just on our way out for lunch. Maybe we'll catch you and Sarah another time. Nice to meet you."

He heard as well as felt Janice's sharp intake of breath. On his other side, he heard Frank clearing his throat.

"Yeah," Rick mumbled. "Nice meeting you."

Trevor nodded toward Sarah, who he noted was very pretty, although she did talk a little too much for his preference. He made a mental note when the whole fiasco with Frank and Laura was over to get Sarah's phone number. "Have a nice day," he said to Sarah.

Without waiting for either of them to respond, he removed his arm from Janice's waist, picked up her hand, and linked his fingers through hers. "Come on, Shorty. Let's go." Not waiting for a response, he gave a slight tug and led her outside. Frank and Laura followed at a distance.

The second they arrived at Frank's car, Janice yanked her hand away. "Shorty? And what did you think—"

He placed his index finger in front of his lips. "Shh. Here they come."

On the way to the restaurant, conversation in the backseat of the car was even more stilted than on the way to church.

Trevor didn't mind. The silence gave him time to think.

He stared absentmindedly out the car window as they drove to the restaurant, unable to believe what he'd done. He'd issued a nonverbal warning to Rick—and to any other male in the vicinity—to keep away from Janice.

He'd acted like some macho jerk, publicly staking his territory.

And he'd done it in God's house.

Trevor squeezed his eyes shut. The only way he could justify his actions would be that he had to show any man who might be interested in Janice that she was taken. He had to perpetuate the illusion that they were dating so they could continue with their mutual mission with Frank and Laura.

He didn't care about himself, but this instance made him realize that he hadn't been fair to Janice. Rick seemed like a pretty decent guy. He appeared to be truly interested in Janice—interested enough that his sister had acted as a matchmaker for him, preplanned or not. Trevor couldn't tell if Janice was interested in return, but she hadn't exactly turned Rick away. She certainly appeared to be enjoying Rick's company.

A pang of guilt settled in his gut. He had prevented Janice from seeking the companionship of someone who might come to love her someday for real. Trevor knew he had come across too strong. By doing so, he had caused Rick to look weak in Janice's eyes, and that was wrong. Because he couldn't tell Rick he wasn't really dating Janice, there was nothing he could do, but he did know that he would have to apologize to Janice. With some luck, when they finally managed to convince Frank and Laura to either postpone or hopefully call off the wedding, maybe enough time would have passed for Rick to be able to face Janice again. If he was still interested. Trevor hoped he hadn't scared Rick off permanently.

When the car came to a stop, Trevor forced himself to stop thinking about Rick and start thinking about the reason he'd made such an effort to show the world that he and Janice were an item.

Frank and Laura joined hands as they walked into the restaurant. Janice wouldn't come near him, and he couldn't blame her. However, he had worked too hard to arrange for this time they were to be spending together so they could talk in a non-threatening environment. He couldn't allow his mishandling of the situation with Rick to spoil it.

He would take his lumps later. For now, they had more important things to deal with.

While they waited for a table, he shuffled Janice to the side to speak as privately as possible amongst the crowd in the restaurant's lobby.

"We have to talk." He almost asked why she was mad at him, but he couldn't bring himself to do it. Besides, he already knew the answer. Instead, he tried to think of something to say that would calm her down. It didn't take a rocket scientist to see how she felt. Her whole body was stiff. Behind her glasses, her brown eyes absolutely flashed. She wasn't just a little mad at him. She was furious.

Before he could think of the right thing to say, she leaned toward him. He tried not to cringe.

"You called me 'Shorty,' " she ground out between her teeth.

Trevor blinked, then stepped back as he looked down at her. He was six feet tall, and judging from the height difference, taking into account her footwear, he figured Janice was only five foot two. She *was* short. It was a fact that couldn't be denied. "It was supposed to be an endearment. . . ." He let his voice trail off.

Janice crossed her arms over her chest and glared up at him. "Oh? Really? Would calling an overweight person 'fatty' be termed an endearment? Or because I wear glasses, would 'four eyes' also be an endearment, in your estimation? Should I be flattered that you address me by my most prominent physical fault, something I can't do anything about?"

Trevor stiffened from head to toe. He had been teased relentlessly as a child about his big nose because that was the problem everyone could see. Through his struggles in school, often the teasing about his big nose had been the straw that broke the camel's back. No one but his mother knew how often as a young child he'd come home crying. As a teen, to his dismay, to top everything off his nose grew proportionally to his height. With the years, his fellow schoolmates became better at inventing creative insults. Short of plastic surgery, his big nose was the one thing he couldn't hide. This was the way God had made him. Fortunately, now no one ever bugged him about his big nose, and it was a welcome relief, although he was sure many people thought about it.

"Uh. . .I never thought of it that way. I'm sorry." He let the silence hang until he finished fighting his personal demons of his youth. When he finally returned his attention to Janice's face, her expression had softened. He could see on her face that she'd forgiven him.

He cleared his throat. "I thought we should talk about Rick."

Her eyebrows rose. "Rick? Why do you want to talk about him? That was quite a little performance you put on, by the way. If I didn't know better, I would have thought we were together. You were quite convincing. I hope you can handle the gossip. You should have seen everyone watching you. It was really funny. Oh. They just called our table. Come on."

Their time together progressed much the same as their pizza dinner the night before. Together, they did manage to point out a few things to Frank and Laura that made the outing a worthwhile expedition, but for the moment, nothing changed. Not that he expected them to realize how wrong they were for each other in only one day. Trevor only hoped and prayed that they'd planted the first of many seeds today that would make them think about things more realistically as time went on.

When they were done and the bill and tip were paid for, Trevor was pleased that Janice and Laura invited him and Frank to their house for the afternoon. It was another opportunity Trevor couldn't turn down.

He stayed with Frank in the living room while the women went into the kitchen to make coffee. He realized too late that he should have offered to go into the kitchen with Janice, as he wanted to talk to her privately about a few things that were said at lunchtime. He didn't need more time with Frank. They lived together and saw each other every day.

Frank's voice jolted him out of his thoughts.

"What did you think of Laura's church? It sure is different, isn't it?"

Without thinking, Trevor's hand went up to his throat, to pat the knot on his missing tie. "Yeah. It sure is. And you've already decided to get married and attend there, huh?"

Frank smiled and gazed out the window. "Yeah. It's big, but I figure I'll get used to it."

Other than the informal atmosphere, Trevor couldn't see anything else wrong with the church. The congregation all appeared sincere. Despite his personal preferences, he knew there was benefit to getting together with a large group to worship God. Therefore, he couldn't say anything.

He decided to change the subject because Laura and Janice had returned.

Frank covered Laura's hand as soon as she sat down beside him. Fortunately for Trevor, he'd sat in the armchair, so he didn't have to sit beside Janice.

He looked across the room to Frank and Laura, who were all snuggled up. "Have you two decided on a guest list or anything?" Trevor asked. "And what about the size of the wedding party? As far as I know, Janice and I are it."

Laura smiled at Frank as she answered him. "I thought we should have a small wedding. You know. Something private. Sunday is the time for a large gathering."

Frank's eyebrows rose. "I know guys aren't supposed to care about stuff like this, but I've always wanted a big wedding. This is a celebration of the start of our new lives together. I wanted to invite lots of people."

Trevor tried not to gloat. Here was something else they disagreed on. He and Janice exchanged sly glances.

"You know, Laura," Janice said, folding her hands demurely in her lap, "this is something you should have agreed on first. It doesn't look like you discussed the guest list either before you booked the church."

Frank and Laura gazed lovingly into each other's eyes. The last time Trevor had seen such sappy expressions was in an old B movie an old girlfriend once forced him to watch.

"That's okay," Laura said as she sighed airily. "We can meet in the middle. Isn't marriage all about compromise?"

Trevor nodded. Of course he knew compromise was a necessary ingredient for a successful marriage. However, he'd always thought that the more a couple agreed on in the first place, the less compromise was necessary and, therefore, the better the chances that the relationship would survive the test of time.

"Okay," Frank said. "I had figured on five hundred guests and four attendants."

Laura's eyes widened. "Are you counting Trev and Janice? So that means one bridesmaid and one groomsman besides them?"

Frank shook his head. "No, I mean besides them. Four attendants each."

"But I didn't want a big wedding party. How about this? If you reduce the number of attendants, I won't mind more guests."

"How many guests?"

"I only wanted a hundred guests. But you can have fifty more guests for each less attendant."

"Each?"

"Total."

"Then three hundred guests, two attendants. Each."

"Only Janice and Trevor, you can have three hundred and fifty."

"Deal."

"Done."

They shook hands, then turned and smiled at Trevor.

Trevor wanted to shake his head. They'd reduced the planning for a wedding to a bartering exchange. This wasn't exactly the way he'd pictured a couple in love discussing their upcoming wedding ceremony.

Trevor cleared his throat. "Have you at least decided where

you're going to live when you get married?"

Frank nodded. "We'll rent an apartment downtown, close to our jobs. A high-rise."

Laura's smile disappeared. "But I wanted a house in the suburbs. With a big yard and a garden."

Frank shrugged his shoulders. "We'll have lots of time to discuss that later."

Laura shrugged her shoulders. "I suppose. . ."

Frank turned to Janice and smiled. "That coffee smells great. Is it ready yet?"

four

Janice stood. She glanced at Trevor, hoping he would follow her, but Laura jumped to her feet instead and accompanied her into the kitchen.

Janice didn't know what to do. It appeared that Laura and Frank were going to have their first argument about the wedding in the company of herself and Trevor. This was exactly the opportunity they were striving for. Not only one, but two obvious disagreements had risen to the surface.

Now was the perfect time to gently point out to Laura how ill-suited she and Frank were for each other.

But Janice couldn't do it. Laura was her best friend. She wanted to console her friend—to tell her that their disagreement would blow over and that everything would be all right. However, that wasn't what she was supposed to do. Not that she didn't want Laura and Frank to kiss and make up—her ultimate goal was for her friend to be happy. For today, she and Trevor would strive for Laura and Frank to understand their disagreement in the perspective of the big picture.

When Laura and Frank passed the stage of the warm fuzzies, it would take more than a quick smile to solve their issues. When their relationship developed into making choices instead of simply flowing with the attraction, Frank and Laura would never make it. They were just too different, and their needs in a marriage partner too far apart.

She expected Laura to say something about the wedding plans gone askew, but she didn't. Instead, Laura rummaged in the fridge for the cream while Janice poured the coffee into four mugs.

As soon as Laura closed the fridge and stood upright, Janice knew she had to say something, but she didn't know what. She didn't want to rub her friend's face in her failures or her bad choices. Besides, not only Laura's feelings were involved. Frank was also her friend, and she didn't want to hurt him either.

Janice cleared her throat. "Laura, I've been thinking. You two haven't had enough time to plan everything out. You know what I mean. All those nitpicky wedding details. Also, you two really should discuss other important things beyond the wedding. Not only where you want to live but also all the practical day-to-day stuff. Don't you think maybe you should set the wedding back for awhile and work all this stuff out first?"

Laura smiled. "But we did work it out. We only have to make the actual guest lists."

Janice forced herself to smile. She didn't consider the bartering exchange she'd witnessed working it out. Also, Frank never did settle the issue of the downtown apartment. He'd simply dismissed Laura to get the coffee, which rankled Janice.

"But what about where you're going to live? It's important that you both agree."

"I don't care where we live, Silly. We're in love. We'll be happy wherever we are."

"You say that now, but there's more to it than that."

"Not really. Love conquers all, you know."

Janice shook her head. "But love isn't blind, deaf, and dumb, Laura. It's complicated."

Laura picked up the mugs meant for herself and Frank. "Love is only as complicated as you make it. Come on. Before the coffee gets cold."

Balancing two mugs in one hand and a plate of cookies in the other, Janice followed Laura into the living room. Judging from Trevor's expression, she could see whatever reasoning he'd attempted with Frank had netted the same result.

She rested the plate on the coffee table and handed one of the mugs to Trevor.

He sipped the coffee slowly, then sighed. "Thanks. I see

you remembered how I like it."

"It was easy. You take it the same way as I do. Double cream, no sugar."

He nodded. "Frank and I were thinking that it would be fun to do something after work tomorrow. You interested?"

She wasn't really, but Trevor mouthed a "please" at her when no one else was looking at him. She had no idea what he had in mind. However, neither of them had made any progress in their quest so far. "Sure, that would be nice," she said, trying to smile and make it look like she meant it. "What have you got in mind?"

"I dunno. Something we can do together. I don't feel like sitting in a restaurant. I want to do something. You think of what we can do."

Her mind went blank, especially with the three of them staring at her. "Well," she mumbled, letting her voice trail off while she rested her hand under her chin and tapped her cheek with her index finger. "How about bowling?"

Trevor blinked and continued to stare at her. "Bowling? I was thinking more of wide-open spaces."

Laura's face lit up. "Bowling! What a wonderful idea! I haven't been bowling for years."

Frank turned to stare at Trevor. "Yeah. That's a good idea. I love bowling."

Trevor's eyes widened. "I haven't been bowling since junior high school. But if that's what everybody else wants, I guess I can do that."

Laura nodded and glanced at the clock. "You know, it's nearly five o'clock. Do you guys want to stay for supper? I think we can scrape something together. Maybe I should put the cookies away."

Trevor rested one hand on his stomach, which Janice thought kind of cute. He smiled brightly. "I'd love a home-cooked meal."

Frank turned to him. "What are you talking about? You cook pretty good, and we eat at home all the time. There's nothing wrong with the stuff we eat."

Trevor grinned. "Food always tastes better when someone else makes it, no matter what it is."

Janice nodded. "I know. Laura does most of the cooking here, and everything she makes definitely tastes better than my cooking."

Frank nodded too. "Trev does pretty much all of the cooking at our place."

Janice didn't know how it happened, but somehow Laura and Trevor disappeared into the kitchen, leaving her alone in the living room with Frank. Not that she felt like cooking, but she had thought this would have been a good opportunity to talk to Trevor. To her surprise, they returned, both grinning and winking at each other, to announce that they were going to make a surprise for supper. They instructed Janice and Frank to stay in the living room until they were done and disappeared as quickly as they had come.

Janice gritted her teeth. Again, another opportunity to talk to Trevor in private where they could come up with another plan had been lost.

Still, if she had to see something as good instead of as a loss, she could take this as an opportunity to talk to Frank. She hoped that Trevor was doing the same with Laura.

She started out by talking about the things she had in common with Laura, then steered the conversation over to Laura's hobbies and choices of entertainment. It came as no surprise that many of them were news to Frank. For recreation, Laura enjoyed crafts and other sedentary pastimes. Laura's idea of strenuous exercise was a trip through the mall during the holiday season. Laura's only form of outdoor recreation consisted of a walk through the park if the weather was just right.

On the other hand, Frank enjoyed more strenuous pursuits such as skiing and cycling. Unfortunately, he didn't seem to find anything wrong with the fact that Laura didn't share his interests. He only laughed and said that if one of her hobbies was cooking, then he had no complaints.

The whole time Janice tried to explain to Frank that Laura wasn't about to suddenly take up hang gliding, she heard Trevor and Laura laughing and goofing around in the kitchen.

By the time they returned, Janice could barely believe that nearly an hour had passed. She'd tried her best with Frank, but one look at Trevor and Laura told her they hadn't talked about anything important or done anything except cook supper and make a mess in the kitchen.

"Whatever you're cooking smells great," she said, trying her best to be gracious. Not that she wasn't telling the truth. She didn't know what Trevor was like in the kitchen, but she knew Laura was a great cook. Laura was just as creative in the kitchen as she was with her crafts, while Janice had two left thumbs.

"I'm not telling what we made, but you'll probably guess pretty soon."

Janice tried to think of what they had on hand, but she wasn't sure since Laura usually did most of the grocery shopping. "Sorry, I haven't a clue."

Trevor checked his wristwatch. "You don't have time to guess anyway. We still have stuff to do, and supper will be ready in ten minutes. Laura told me it's your favorite thing."

Janice gritted her teeth. They weren't supposed to be discussing her favorite things. They were supposed to be comparing Laura and Frank's favorite things.

Everyone was watching her, probably expecting her to immediately guess what they had made. "You made chocolate chip cookies for supper?"

"Well, maybe your second-favorite thing."

Immediately, she knew they'd made lasagna. "You're kidding. Right?"

"Wrong."

"I thought it smelled like lasagna for awhile, but there's something else."

Trevor grinned. "We fried an onion to mask the smell of the lasagna. Pretty smart, huh?"

Now she knew what at least some of the laughter had been about.

She could have mentioned something Trevor could have done that would have been smarter, but she chose to bite her tongue. In silence, she followed everyone else into the kitchen. Immediately Janice and Frank sat down. Trevor and Laura brought everything to the table.

They prayed together and began to eat. Janice had never tasted such delicious lasagna in her life. Not only had they made a big salad to go with the lasagna, they had also taken a loaf of bread and cooked it with garlic butter. Everyone laughed at the accompanying side dish of sautéed mushrooms and onions.

"Pretty good, huh?" Frank mumbled around his mouthful.

Laura beamed. "Trevor was the head cook here today. It was a real treat to let someone else take charge in my kitchen. And now I know his secret ingredient. Next time, I'm going to use it."

Janice nodded while she swallowed her mouthful. "Laura does most of the cooking here, in case you can't tell." She turned to Trevor. She didn't want to say anything about how surprised she was, not only that he could cook but that he did it so well. Still, she couldn't not say anything. He'd done too good of a job to let it go. "This is great, Trevor. My compliments to the chef."

"You're welcome. But don't thank me too much. We did it together as a team."

When everyone was so overstuffed they couldn't eat another bite, they all rose from the table.

Instead of leaving the room, Trevor helped himself to another glass of milk. "By the way, we've already discussed it, and since Laura and I did the cooking, you and Frank are doing the dishes."

Janice surveyed the mess. Beyond a total lack of culinary talent, this was the biggest reason she avoided cooking any more than she had to. Usually, the quality of the meal was inversely proportional to the mess produced to create it. More important than the dishes, she wanted to talk to Trevor, not spend more time with Frank. But after Trevor had made such a wonderful dinner, she could hardly refuse.

She shrugged her shoulders. "I guess so. It's the least I can do after all your hard work. I had no idea you were such a good cook."

Trevor grinned and placed one hand over his heart. "My daddy always told me that the way to a woman's heart is through her stomach."

Every thought in Janice's head deserted her. All she could do was stare at him.

Frank cleared his throat behind her. "Remember when I washed your car for you last week?"

Trevor glanced behind her to Frank, then shrugged his shoulders. "I think I owe Frank a favor, and he's calling me on it. I guess this means that you and I are doing the dishes, and Frank is off the hook. I don't mind. This gives us a chance to be alone together, although I could think of a few things I'd rather be doing alone with you other than the dishes."

It took a few seconds for what Trevor said to sink in. She opened her mouth to ask him what in the world he was alluding to when Frank spoke up.

"That doesn't get any argument from me. Come on, Laura. Let's go."

Frank and Laura disappeared in seconds flat.

Janice tapped her foot, crossed her arms, and glared daggers at Trevor. "What in the world are you trying to do? Do you know what that sounded like?"

Trevor turned his back to her and returned the milk carton to the fridge. "Relax, Janice," he said from within the fridge. "I'm teasing you. We're supposed to be dating, remember? Don't you think that's what couples should do? Get away from the crowd to be alone every now and then?"

"Frank and Laura aren't a crowd," she said to his back as he continued to move things around in the fridge. Nor were they really a "couple." Still, being alone with Trevor in the kitchen was exactly what she wanted in the first place. She convinced herself that it was only the rebel within her that no longer wanted it to happen.

She cleared her throat. "We have to talk."

He left the fridge door partway open, picked up the pan of leftover lasagna from the counter, and worked it into the empty space he'd made. Janice heard more banging and shuffling as he attempted to make more room for the large pan.

His voice came out muffled as he spoke. "Hey. You've got a chocolate bar ditched in here."

"What I've got put away in a safe place in my fridge is none of your business. What's supposed to be your business is this issue with Frank and Laura. Will you get out of there?"

Slowly, he backed up and straightened. As he turned around, he waved the chocolate bar that was supposed to be in the fridge back and forth in front of her. He grinned and quirked up one eyebrow. "Mmm. My favorite. If you loved me, you'd share."

Janice opened her mouth, but no sound came out. Before she said something she knew she'd regret, she stomped forward and grabbed her chocolate bar out of his hand. She straightened her glasses on her nose, narrowed her eyes, and glared up at him. "I don't know what you think you're doing but stop it. We have important stuff to talk about."

His focus remained glued to the chocolate bar the whole time she reprimanded him. She whipped it behind her back.

Trevor's posture sagged, and he lost his smile. "All I wanted was one little bite. But that's okay. I have three sisters. I know from experience what happens when a man comes between a woman and her chocolate bar."

All the fight left her. She held the bar out to him and sighed. "If you need it that bad, take it. I have a feeling we don't have anything to talk about, anyway. I heard you and Laura goofing around the whole time you were making supper. Didn't you think that it would have been a good time to talk to her about Frank?"

Trevor removed the chocolate bar from her hands, tore open the wrapper, and took a bite. He closed his eyes as he chewed slowly, savoring it like he hadn't tasted chocolate for years. As he swallowed, he opened his eyes and smiled. "This is my favorite kind. You want some?" He tore back the wrapper but didn't actually give it to her. Instead, he held it out as if she should take a bite while it was still in his hand.

Janice shook her head. At her indication that she didn't want any, he took a second bite, then proceeded to talk with a mouthful.

"I may not have directly pointed out how wrong they are for each other, but I was working on something else. I've known her for a couple of years but only as a casual acquaintance. We don't really know each other very well, at least not where it counts for true friendship. Before she trusts me, she's got to learn that I'm on her side. Then she'll take what I say more to heart." He paused and pointed at her with the half-eaten chocolate bar. "You know, like witnessing to someone you don't know that well. First you have to earn the right to be heard."

"I never thought of it that way. That's probably a good idea. But I did have a nice talk with Frank. Even if I couldn't get him to agree with me on the whole thing, he did admit that he and Laura don't share many common interests."

"I guess that's a start. But you know him better than I know her. You at least knew where to start."

"Yes. And speaking of starting, we should start these dishes, or we're going to be stuck here in the kitchen all night. Since this is my house and I know where everything goes, you wash, and I'll dry."

Trevor tucked the remainder of the chocolate bar into the torn wrapper and laid it on the counter. He then rolled up his sleeves and began rinsing the dirty dishes that were stacked beside the sink. As Janice gathered everything else that needed to be washed, she watched him, glancing out the corner of her eye.

Until today, every other time she'd met him, she'd always considered Trevor to be the quiet type. Today she'd seen a side of him she'd never seen before. She'd been especially surprised by his little performance with Rick. Once Trevor warmed up, he really wasn't very quiet at all. In fact, she wondered if it would be hard to turn him off once he got started.

Also, once he got started and opened up, his warm smile changed his whole countenance. He may not have been handsome in a classical sense, especially since he had such a large nose, but when he smiled, his smile came all the way from his heart.

This morning, she couldn't believe it when he'd arrived for church all dressed up. In all the other times she'd met him, he'd been wearing jeans and a comfortably worn T-shirt, like her. Today, in the pristine monotone jacket, shirt, and pants ensemble, she couldn't believe the difference. The contrast between the dark clothes and his blond hair came across as quite striking, adding to his overall appeal.

Apparently, clothes did make the man.

She'd meant to talk about Frank and Laura, but as they worked together to wash and dry dishes and clean up the kitchen, they talked about everything except their friends. He told her wryly how even though it wasn't what he was used to, her church service had pleasantly surprised him. It pleased her that he enjoyed it. Before she realized what she'd done, she agreed to attend the service at his church with him the following week.

When they were done, they joined Frank and Laura in the living room. Instead of talking, the four of them sat together on the couch and watched the second half of a television drama. Part of Janice told her that they were wasting the evening, but another part of her just wanted to relax and enjoy the quiet time without pressure.

At the end of the program, Frank stood. "I think it's time to be going. Everyone has to get up early for work tomorrow."

Trevor rose to follow as Frank and Laura walked outside,

and Janice rose to follow Trevor. One step beyond the doorway, Trevor stopped. Not realizing he'd stopped, Janice walked into his back, bumping him forward. He tottered slightly but corrected his balance as he spun around and grabbed the railing with one hand.

As he faced her, Janice covered her mouth with her hands. Her heart pounded at the thought of what almost happened. Through her carelessness, she'd almost sent him flying down the steps. She would have been the cause of him breaking his neck. She may not exactly have liked him, but she certainly didn't want to kill him. "I'm so sorry!" she squeaked out with her heart in her throat. "Are you okay?"

Her breath caught as she realized that they were only inches apart. He couldn't back up, or he would go down the steps for real. She could have backed up, but her feet seemed glued to the porch.

His voice came out in a low rumble. "Don't worry. I'm fine. Are you okay?"

She nodded. "Why did you stop?"

The words barely out of her mouth, she glanced past Trevor to see Frank and Laura wrapped in each other's arms, locked in a kiss.

"Oh," she mumbled. "Never mind."

Trevor broke out into a wide grin. "We're supposed to be officially dating, you know. Good night, Janice." Before she had a chance to speak and bid him good night, he closed his eyes, placed his hands behind his back, leaned slightly forward, puckered his lips, and made a loud smooching sound in the air.

Her mind went blank, and she broke out into a cold sweat. "Get real," she hissed. Miraculously, her feet became unglued from the porch floor. Before he could respond, she backed up into the house and pushed the door closed inches from his face.

She stood staring at the closed door, unable to believe what she'd just done or what had nearly happened.

Trevor's laughter echoed through the heavy wooden door.

Her mind raced as she tried to think of what she should do. Certainly, she had no intention of opening the door and talking to him after this. Nor could she afford to take the chance that he would open the door and come in. The clock above the fireplace ticked, nagging her that it wouldn't be much longer until Laura would return.

Janice didn't want to be near the door when it opened in case he was still there, so she turned and ran. Not thinking of where she was going, she found herself in the kitchen. And since she was in the kitchen, she stared straight at the fridge, which held her emergency chocolate bar.

She had the fridge door partway open when she remembered that Trevor had absconded her secret stash after supper. However, she didn't recall him actually finishing it.

She turned her head, and sure enough, the half-eaten chocolate bar sat on the counter near the sink, all nicely wrapped up and tucked to the side.

Praising God for small miracles, she pushed the fridge door closed with a muffled bang. Without delay, she strode across the kitchen, scooped up the chocolate bar, and ran into her bedroom. In the privacy of her room, she nibbled away at the remainder, savoring it bite by bite, letting the soothing chocolate calm her shattered nerves. However, she knew that from this moment on, she would never be able to think of her favorite chocolate bar without picturing Trevor nibbling at it and waving it in her face between bites.

She stared through the window into the dark night for a few seconds, then yanked the curtain shut.

Tomorrow was another day. Unfortunately, it was another day she would see Trevor Halliday.

five

Trevor lay on his back, staring up at the dark ceiling. Not for the first time, he turned his head to check the glowing green numbers of the clock radio.

Four twenty-seven. In only three hours he had to get up for work, and he'd barely slept.

He squeezed his eyes shut, but the self-imposed blackness couldn't stop thoughts of Janice from cascading through his mind.

In an attempt to block Janice out of his consciousness, he draped his forearm over his eyes. It didn't help. In his mind's eye, he could still see her.

He couldn't believe how he'd behaved. He couldn't say he was trying to be funny, although he had to admit that he'd certainly enjoyed himself in an odd kind of way. He would never have foreseen himself deliberately provoking a woman, yet that was exactly what he'd done. He couldn't remember the last time he'd laughed so hard as when she'd closed the door in his face. The entire way home, Frank had caught him still snickering about it. Trevor was at a loss to explain why, because he didn't understand it himself.

Now, in the silence of the night, the more he thought about it, the less funny his actions became.

He'd met her many times before Frank and Laura's engagement, but he'd never paid her much notice. Not that there was anything specifically wrong with Janice. It was just that between the ordinary brown hair, the ordinary brown eyes, her total lack of height, and the quiet and studious demeanor which her functional glasses only magnified, she'd never done anything to make him take notice.

Today, though, he'd seen the fire in her eyes, and it

mesmerized him. In spending so much time so close to her over the past few days, he did something he'd never done before. He'd looked at her. *Really* looked at her. He'd seen past everything that made her appearance ordinary and beyond everything she did to fade into the background. Her eyes truly were the windows to her soul. Her thoughts and reactions to everything he'd done couldn't have been clearer if the words were written in neon pen across her forehead.

Janice was doing the exact opposite to him as Frank and Laura were doing to each other. Frank and Laura only put their best foot forward with each other. For whatever reason, they chose not to show anything that might disturb the status quo of their relationship. The end result, intentional or not, was that they were not being honest with each other in their actions—or their responses.

Through Janice's unpretentious reactions, Trevor couldn't help but see how she felt about everything he'd done.

She was furious when he called her Shorty, even though he'd originally misjudged the reason for her anger as his leading Rick to believe they were seriously together. But the more he thought about it and the more he came to know her, he realized that she had accepted all facets of letting Frank and Laura believe they were truly a couple. Looking at the big picture, the rest of their little universe had to also perceive them as a couple. She had already accepted that for the time being, she wouldn't be pursuing relationships with other men, regardless of who started it, as part of the package. Not only did she not have a problem with him acting like a jealous boyfriend, she'd expected it. He realized he hadn't given her enough credit.

He also saw in her face that she thought he was too stuffy when he arrived for church appropriately dressed. Normally, he would have been annoyed for being judged like that. However, in the end she'd been right. He would have felt very self-conscious if he'd arrived at her church in his true Sunday best while everyone else around him, with the exception of her boss, wore clothes fit for little better than a Sunday picnic.

After lunch, when they'd returned to her house, her annoyance when he was joking with Laura in the kitchen couldn't have been more obvious. But by that time, he'd been just as annoyed with her as she was with him. The woman never let up on anything. He wanted to take a little break and relax. She didn't. All he wanted to do was enjoy a good meal, especially when he'd worked so hard to prepare it. She remained steadfast and focused on the reason they were together in the first place, which was to straighten out their friends. Nothing more and nothing less.

Then he'd taken her chocolate bar. The reason he'd taken it wasn't because he wanted it so bad. By that time, he simply wanted to see what she would do when she lost something, because she'd won at everything else all day.

Without specifically calling them arguments, she'd beaten him on every issue. She'd won the argument about his clothes. She'd certainly convinced him that calling her Shorty had not been an endearment. She'd also been right about him goofing off with Laura in the kitchen, regardless of his justifications for his behavior.

He was being childish, but he wanted to, for once, get one up on her. He wanted to see what would happen if she lost a small battle in her quest to win the war. He'd chosen his wording for getting the chocolate bar from her in such a way that she couldn't say no. Then he'd made a grand show of savoring and enjoying every bite.

Somewhere in the middle of his little performance, something changed. At first he'd thought he was only teasing her, watching her watching him eat her treat—which she'd surrendered to him. By the time he got halfway through, he'd felt so guilty he couldn't finish.

Trevor rolled over and buried his face in the pillow. At the time, he hadn't really thought about why he'd wanted to challenge Janice. Now, after much introspection, the reason behind his actions hit him. It had been more than friendly teasing.

He was measuring her up against Brenda, his ex-girlfriend, comparing them.

He'd once done something similar to tease Brenda, but instead of it being a treasured, hidden treat, he'd made a game of holding back something useless and frivolous—the toy from a fast-food kid's meal, something Brenda couldn't have cared less about. Even though the battle itself was meaningless, she still cared about winning.

He'd previously experienced Brenda's crocodile tears when she wanted to convince him to do things her way. He'd pointedly ignored Frank's jibes about being a sucker and giving in every time Brenda turned on the waterworks. On that occasion, though, she hadn't cried, but he hadn't been prepared for what Brenda did.

At first she had playfully pouted, acting coy and cutesy. When that failed to net the toy, she had gone on to distract him, using his interest in her against him. At the time, he'd had a hopeless crush on her, and she knew it. When she couldn't reach the toy as he held it over his head, Trevor had laughed. But he stopped laughing when she started touching him suggestively. To entice him, she ran her fingers down his cheek and through his hair. Then, when she saw that she was having an effect on him, she started planting little kisses on his chin until he couldn't think. Then, her teasing little kisses moved closer to his mouth, like she was going to kiss him for real. As soon as he lowered his arms to embrace her properly, she snatched the toy from his hand, stepped away, and laughed. The game was over. She'd won. He had been goofing around, but Brenda had been more than serious.

Watching her wave the toy in front of his nose in triumph, everything had come together with shocking clarity. Brenda hadn't kissed him as a sign of affection. She kissed him as a means to get what she wanted—as a tool, even a weapon. She was playing dirty. Knowing how he felt about her, she'd used her feminine charms to make him weak, then used his weakness against him. It hadn't been that she'd managed to take the toy from him that bothered him; it was how she did it. She'd manipulated him with no thought or concern for his emotions or his heart—with a clear conscience. That day had been the end of his relationship with Brenda.

And now, he'd used Janice's chocolate bar against her, teasing her with it in order to test her. He'd dared her, challenged her, yet she'd done the honorable thing, which was nothing.

Realizing how he was testing her and comparing her when she'd done nothing to deserve such treatment made him feel lower than a common earthworm. What started as a game had suddenly turned into something else.

Instead of trying to manipulate him like Brenda would have, with sad eyes and crocodile tears, Janice only stared at him in unmasked disbelief when he'd actually started eating her chocolate bar. He'd seen in her face that she really didn't think he'd do it. Then, in a split second, her face had hardened, and she'd bluntly told him they should have been dealing with the problem at hand, which was Frank and Laura. She never mentioned the candy bar again, everything was back to normal, and they'd started cleaning up the kitchen.

He'd never enjoyed doing dishes before, but the time had gone surprisingly fast as he and Janice completed their chore. He could almost have forgotten that they were only pretending to like each other to fulfill their mutual goal.

He'd tested her twice that evening. Once with the chocolate bar and again at the door as they parted.

He honestly didn't know what would have happened if she had called his bluff and actually kissed him.

Trevor flipped over on his side and pulled his blanket up to his chin. The more he thought about it, the more he thought that Janice wouldn't have kissed him, and she would never kiss him. He didn't know her tremendously well, but well enough to know that Janice would only kiss a man if she meant it, which was as it should be.

Tomorrow, he would figure out how to make things right for taking her chocolate bar and eating it in front of her. Then, all would be well with his soul.

❧

"Good morning, Quinlan Enterprises," Janice singsonged. As she spoke, she knocked over a stack of purchase orders one of the supervisors had just deposited on her desk. She struggled to grab the pile and not let the phone fall from her shoulder where it was precariously balanced.

"Hi, Janice. It's me. Trevor. I hope you don't mind me calling you at work."

"Trevor?" She gulped. The phone slid off her shoulder anyway, and she scrambled to catch it before it hit the floor. Her desk sat alone in the entrance to the office building, but she lowered her voice to a whisper anyway, since it was a personal call. "How did you get my number?"

"I phoned Frank at work, and he phoned Laura at her work and left a message. Then she phoned me back on her coffee break and gave me your number. You won't get in trouble, will you?"

"My boss is really nice, but I can't abuse taking personal calls on company time. What do you want?"

She waited for his reply, which stretched into a long, heavy silence. She wondered what he had to think about so hard before he spoke. While she waited, she glanced up at the clock. It was exactly noon, so it was unlikely that a call would come in to interrupt him once he got started, if he got started. She would have liked to hear that something had transpired from her little talk with Frank the night before. However, the longer the silence dragged on, the less optimistic she became.

Finally, he spoke. "I wanted to know if you were free to go out to lunch with me. How long do you get for your break?"

A knot formed in the pit of her grumbling stomach. She had no idea what could be so important that couldn't be said over the phone or couldn't wait until evening, when they met to go bowling. If it was good news that Frank and Laura were starting to appraise their relationship in a realistic light, Trevor should have just said so. Instead of the encouraging news she hoped she would hear, a cloud of discouragement settled in—maybe the situation had become worse instead of better.

She looked up at the time again. "I get half an hour for lunch, starting at 12:30. I don't know where you work. Are you close by? I'd offer to meet you halfway, but I take the bus to work and leave my car at home."

"It's not too far. Well, maybe it's a little ways away. Okay, I guess it's not that close. I work in the industrial park, and I know that you're downtown. It will probably take me about twenty minutes to get there, which would work if I leave right now."

The sudden silence told her Trevor was waiting for her to accept or decline his invitation.

She looked up at the clock again, calculating his travel time in addition to the length of time they would need to eat. Even if he got an hour for his lunch break, he would still exceed his allotted time allowance.

Now she knew it had to be important.

Janice cleared her throat. "Yes. If you're in a rush, we can grab a quick lunch at the place down the block."

"Great. If you wait out front, I won't have to waste precious time and go into the visitor parking lot. See you at 12:30. Bye."

Janice found herself staring at the handset while the dial tone buzzed. At the sound of footsteps echoing on the tile floor behind her, she fumbled with the phone and hung it up quickly, then returned her attention to her work.

Right on time, Susan arrived to relieve her. Janice dashed outside at the same time as Trevor's car pulled over to the curb in front of the building, in a no parking zone.

She scrambled into his car in three seconds flat, barely fastening the seat belt before the car was once again in motion.

"Did you have to circle around the block, or did I make it?"

He checked over his shoulder as he pulled into the downtown lunch-rush traffic. "I should say I had to circle a few times, but that would be lying. Your timing was perfect. I just got here. Where should we go? I seldom come downtown and never for lunch on a weekday."

Janice pointed straight ahead toward the fast-food restaurant. "There's the place I usually go when I don't bring a lunch. One block that way—on the corner. They have a nice variety, it's fast, and best of all for you, they have ample free parking for customers."

"I'm not going to argue with that. That's a big part of the reason I never come downtown. No parking. And I don't like the crowds."

"I know what you mean. If it weren't for my job, I wouldn't come downtown either. Everything I want is close to home. Why should I go miles and miles for the same thing I can get right next door? I've never considered shopping an adventure."

He nodded and steered the car into the parking lot. Janice pointed to an empty spot, and soon they were standing in line at the counter.

She couldn't wait until they sat down. If what he had to say was so important that he'd gone through such trouble to come all this way, she wanted to know now. "Is Frank starting to change his mind about the wedding yet?" she blurted out, not caring about the proximity of the other people in line around them.

"I don't know. I really haven't talked to him since last night. I don't know what things are like at your place, but on a workday morning, Frank and I kind of grunt at each other as we get ready to run out the door. But he did remind me that we're all going bowling tonight."

She waited for him to say more, but when she turned toward him, he was looking up and reading the menu board.

"It's the same for me and Laura in the morning too. You talked to Laura on the phone today, didn't you? Did she reconsider this thing with Frank?"

He stepped forward with the line as he continued to study the board. "I don't know. She really only had time to give me directions how to get here and your phone number. I don't know if you could call that talking. I'm going to have the number six. What do you want?" He turned and grinned at her. "My treat."

The rest of her question about talking to Laura caught in her throat. Those little crinkles she liked so much were back at the corners of his shining blue eyes. Combined with his heart-stopping smile, the man would have been absolutely great in a toothpaste commercial.

Janice reached up and straightened her glasses, just in case they were crooked. "I always have the number three."

He glanced back up to read her choice. "Aw, you don't need that diet junk. Come on. Have a number six with me." He turned his entire body toward her. Slowly, he reached forward. With a touch so light she barely felt it, he ran his index finger along the back of her wrist. One eyebrow quirked up, and his voice dropped to a low, husky whisper. "Just for today, you can live dangerously."

Janice forced herself to breathe. She didn't know what just happened, but suddenly the danger became more than a high-cholesterol, artery-clogging, mega-calorie, fast-food meal.

She tried to clear her throat, but her voice still came out all funny. "Then I'll have the number five."

Trevor turned to the clerk. "Two number fives, please. And make one of them the super size. With two coffees."

As he fished his wallet out of his back pocket and paid the clerk, Janice kneaded her lower lip between her teeth and watched him. She still couldn't believe this was really happening. She'd lain awake in bed for hours last night, going over and over in her mind how Trevor had stepped between her and Rick at church. Even though it probably wasn't politically correct to act that way, she had secretly been flattered by his actions. She'd never had a man care enough about her to be possessive, and it was a new experience, even if it was only in her mind. One day, in God's timing, a man who would be her perfect mate would cross her path, and she could live happily ever after. Until then, she was stuck with Trevor Halliday and her overactive imagination. Still, even though he wasn't tall, dark, and handsome like Frank, two out of three wasn't bad.

He lifted the tray and tilted his head to one side. "I see an empty table. To the left."

Janice followed him through the small cafeteria-style restaurant. Because she was so short, she always had difficulty finding an empty table. However, Trevor stood nearly a head taller than most of the people present, making her slightly jealous of the advantage his height gave him.

She tucked her purse under her chair while Trevor removed the food from the tray and divided everything between them. After a moment of silence, he said a short and quiet prayer of thanks for the food, and they began to eat.

Trevor nodded once while he chewed. "This is good," he mumbled through the food in his mouth. "Coming here was a great idea."

"Everything here is good. Even the 'lite' meal."

He smiled. "Maybe. But I'm not a rabbit. Men need real food."

She almost started to say that the high-cholesterol mayonnaise blend in his sandwich and deep-fried potatoes on the side didn't exactly qualify as "real food" on a consistent basis, but she stopped herself. Even though he hadn't yet let her know what he wanted to discuss in person, she knew it wasn't to argue about nutrition basics.

"I have no doubt that you're really going to eat all that, plus half of my potatoes, which I won't be able to finish."

He stopped midchew. "Really?" he mumbled, then swallowed. "You don't think you'll finish those? But it's so good. I wish we had a place like this in the industrial park."

"I don't even know where you work or what you do. If we're supposed to be seeing each other, I should probably know what you do for a living."

"It's kind of hard to describe. In my official job description, they call me a mechanical engineer."

"I'm sorry. I don't know what that is."

Trevor shrugged his shoulders and laid his sandwich on the paper plate. "It's a fancy term for a high-tech handyman. I work for V. L. Management, the company who oversees the Valley Lane Industrial Estate. Sometimes I'm an electrician, sometimes I'm a roofer, and sometimes I'm an inspector. Whenever there's a problem with one of the leased buildings, it's my job to go fix it, and if I can't fix it myself, it's my responsibility to contract it out and oversee the project."

"That sounds like an interesting job."

"I guess. No two days are alike, that's for sure. What do you do?"

Janice hunched her shoulders and stared down into her coffee cup. "I'm just the receptionist for Quinlan Enterprises. And I do the accounts payable."

"There's nothing wrong with a desk job. If you like to work inside, it's steady, and you don't mind shuffling paper, that's what counts."

She nodded. "Yes. I like working with people. Basically, I talk on the phone most of the day." Janice grinned.

Trevor returned her smile. "I like working with people too. Except, often they're angry people because the only reason I see them is when something has gone wrong. Like if the roof is leaking and there's a puddle in the lobby. Or in the center of the boss's desk."

Janice listened intently as Trevor entertained her with stories of the interesting and unusual disasters he'd had to deal with in his history as a mechanical engineer. Before she knew it, half an hour had passed—and then some. They abandoned their unfinished fried potatoes and half-cups of coffee and literally ran to Trevor's car. Fortunately, the one-block trip from the restaurant to her office building took less than a minute.

When Trevor stopped at the red light, Janice opened the door to get out. "Don't circle the block. The office is just across the street. I'll just cross at the intersection and run in. You can keep going." She had one foot out of the car before she realized that in all the time they'd spent together, they hadn't discussed whatever it was he came for in the first place. Now, not only was she returning late, Trevor's half-hour break was over by more than double, and he still had a twenty-minute drive ahead of him.

She exited the car but didn't close the door. Resting her hands on the roof of the car, she leaned in to talk to him. "I guess I'll see you tonight at the bowling alley," she said.

"Yeah. At seven?"

She glanced up at the light. The cross street's light had turned amber. Her time was up. She nodded. "Seven sounds good."

As she started to back up, Trevor leaned toward her, over the top of the stick shift. "Wait!" he called out. "I have something for you." He reached into a bag between the seats, pulled out a chocolate bar, and handed it to her. "I got this for you. See you later."

She slammed the door closed just as the light turned green.

Janice stood at the curb, staring at the chocolate bar in her hand. It was her favorite kind. The kind Trevor had half eaten last night.

She raised her head and watched Trevor's car as he drove down the street and turned the corner.

She still had no idea why he'd come.

When the light changed, she ran across the street and into her office building. Whatever the reason, she had no choice but to wait until seven o'clock and hope for the best at the bowling alley.

six

"At least I hit something last time, which was better than you did."

"Yeah," Trevor mumbled back to Laura as they watched Janice steadying her bowling ball while she took aim. "She's pretty good, isn't she?"

"Yes. She was in the bowling league where she works last year, so she used to bowl a lot."

Trevor watched Janice do some strange little dance as she pranced to the line, ending with a quick hop before she released the ball, sending it in a straight path down the lane. With an echoing bang, the ball knocked down six pins on her first shot.

He thought she bowled like Fred Flintstone, but then again, she had nearly double his score.

"Bet she gets a spare," Laura said, leaning closer to him so he could hear over the din.

"Probably," he muttered.

Laura then leaned into Frank and ran her hand up and down his arm. "But Frank got another strike last time."

Frank didn't reply. He just turned to Laura and smiled.

"Frank has been bowling in a league for three years," Trevor muttered. "He should be good."

Once again, Trevor watched Janice as she watusied to the line, did her little hippity-hop thing, and sent the ball on its trajectory. The clatter and talking and banging coming from the other lanes continued on, but their own group remained silent as they mentally cheered Janice's ball to success.

At the last second, the ball curved, missing the mark by a fraction of an inch. Three pins went flying. The last one tottered back and forth, causing everyone to hold their breath, trying to will it to fall over. The wobbling slowed and stopped. The last pin remained tauntingly upright.

Trevor smiled as in his mind's eye he pictured himself walking up the long wooden lane and personally kicking the pin down, just so Janice could have scored a spare.

He cleared his throat, his face solemn by the time Janice turned around. "Better luck next time," he called out.

Frank stood and retrieved his ball while Janice approached and sat down at the bench. "I didn't know Frank was this good," she said.

Trevor nodded. "Yeah. He's got his own ball and everything. Last year he got a trophy when his team won some kind of tournament."

"No wonder he was so anxious to go bowling."

He glanced over to Laura, whose attention was totally fixed on Frank as he took aim. Trevor leaned closer to Janice, hoping he could speak quietly, yet still be heard over the racket around them. "Speaking of bowling, how in the world could you come up with an idea like this? The reason we were supposed to get together in the first place was to talk to them, to have them get to know each other better and identify their conflicting interests and personality traits. This place is so noisy and distracting we haven't said a word about anything important, nor are we likely to."

She leaned closer as she spoke, also lowering her voice as the clatter around them continued. "You wanted me to come up with something we could all do together."

"But you were supposed to think of something quiet and romantic!"

In the blink of an eye she turned her face toward his, not giving him time to move or respond. Her face was so close they could almost rub noses. He blinked a few times and managed to focus beyond the reflection of the overhead lights in her glasses. For the first time, he realized her eyes weren't completely brown but were flecked with minute quantities of some kind of olive green.

Her eyes narrowed. "This was the best I could come up with on short notice," she ground out sharply. "I couldn't think with everybody staring at me like that. I'm not a mind reader. If you wanted to do something specific, you should have said so in the first place."

The close proximity made it difficult to maintain his focus. As her face blurred, he had two choices. He could either back up a few inches to see properly, or he could close his eyes. . . and kiss her.

Trevor backed up and shook his head.

"And another thing. You all keep talking about tomorrow night, but I have no idea what it is you've got planned. The other day you said something about a blue dress, and I don't even own a blue dress. You better not have planned something late, either, because we all have to get up for work in the morning."

Trevor shook his head again and held up one palm in the air to silence her. "Relax, Janice. I only suggested we go out to dinner—a nice little place I know about that's quiet and has relatively private tables. I thought it would be nice if you and Laura wore dresses. You know, like a date."

"What makes you think that I'd wear a dress out on a date? I don't even wear a dress to work. You already know I don't wear a dress to church. I own exactly two dresses, neither of which have been worn in a very long time, and neither of them is blue."

Glancing out the corner of his eye, he saw that no pins remained upright in the lane. Frank had turned around and was returning to take a seat, meaning it was Trevor's turn to bowl.

He stood, then leaned down to Janice. "If you don't wear a dress on a date, what do you wear?"

"Just the same thing I always wear, either jeans and a matching top, or whatever I wore to work. I don't fuss and play with my hair either. What you see is what you get."

Behind him, Frank cleared his throat. "Come on, Trev. Your

turn," he called from the scorekeeper's chair. "Quit yapping and start bowling."

Absently, Trevor selected a ball. He stepped into the center of the approach to the lane, wiggled his fingers into the holes of the bowling ball, and took aim. While he was supposed to be concentrating on the pins, Janice's words echoed in his mind.

What she said was truer than she probably realized. The woman didn't appear to put on airs for anyone or anything, even to go so far as to not even dress up for church. Of course God accepted everyone as they came to Him in every aspect of their lives; however, Trevor thought a woman should be a little different when it came to men. Not that he was anyone special that she should dress up for him, but every other woman he'd dated had always put her best foot forward and tried to impress him, at least when they first started dating.

Again, he thought of Brenda. Every time they went out, Brenda had worn nice clothes, and her hair had been perfect, usually with some frilly thing tucked into her curls. Brenda's tastefully applied makeup had always been just right. So far, he couldn't remember Janice ever wearing makeup, except for a little light-colored stuff on her eyelids when he'd picked her up for lunch. He remembered once bumping into Brenda unexpectedly at the grocery store late at night. She'd been embarrassed to have him see her without makeup, even though he'd seen nothing wrong with her, especially considering the time and where they were.

The more he thought about it, the more he realized he would have liked seeing what he was getting with Brenda a lot sooner. He'd only had a superficial view of her—it took quite a bit longer to see her heart, deep down, where she kept everything hidden. He'd gone out with her for a few months before he realized she had a hidden agenda behind much of what she did. Because she had pretended to be someone she was not, it had taken awhile for him to figure her out.

The complete opposite of Brenda was Janice. Everything she thought was as plain as the nose on her face, every opinion bluntly expressed with no guesswork needed. Her home was functional, and she conducted her life in a similar manner. The woman even took the bus to work instead of taking advantage of the freedom and comfort of her car. He thought she could take a few lessons on being at least a little mysterious for a man, unless she planned on being single all her life.

Trevor gave his head a mental shake. He wasn't there to think about Brenda or analyze Janice. He was, unfortunately, there to bowl, and he wanted to get it over with.

He positioned himself at the foot of the bowling lane and sucked in a deep breath. He exhaled, walked in a nice, simple straight line, took a simple aim, and let the ball go. Instead of traveling down the lane in a straight line, the ball curved in a big arc to the left, visibly spinning as it rolled. Then, halfway down the lane, just when he thought the ball would drop into the gutter, it started curving to the right. By the time the ball reached the pins, it knocked down only one, the one on the far right.

Three loud groans echoed behind him.

Frank called out, "I can see why you haven't bowled since junior youth group days, Trev! You're pathetic!"

The reason he hadn't been bowling since junior youth group days was because he hated bowling. It naturally followed that he wasn't very good, but he didn't want his failures announced to the entire population of the bowling alley.

Trevor turned around, about to tell Frank so, but as he did, Janice jumped to her feet.

"Stop that, Frank. He just needs to develop a better delivery."

Trevor could tell that Janice was about to show him how she thought he should bowl. In front of everyone. He didn't care how he bowled. He just wanted to finish the game so they could leave.

He raised both palms in the air as she approached. Janice's rented bowling shoes made a squeaking sound on the polished wooden floor as she skidded to a halt.

"Forget it," he said. "Even though you bowl better than me,

there's no way you're going to get me to do it like that."

She crossed her arms over her chest. "And what's wrong with the way I bowl?"

He raised one hand and walked two fingers in the air. "That little thing you do."

"What do you mean, 'thing'?"

Trevor gritted his teeth. Without another word, he turned around, grabbed one of the bowling balls, positioned himself at the beginning of the runway, or whatever they called it, and prepared to roll the ball.

He glanced briefly over his shoulder. "You bowl like this." As he made his way up the lane, he swiveled his hips from side to side while making short little steps, waggling the ball in front of him as he walked. When he got right to the line, he imitated Janice's dancing little two-step jump, drew the ball back to wind up, and pitched it forward while standing on one foot, making sure to flex his wrist the same way Janice did, just as he let the ball go.

He didn't even wait for it to hit the pins. Trevor twirled around.

Frank was laughing so hard Trevor didn't know how Frank stayed on the seat without falling down. Beside Frank, Laura sat stiff as a board, her eyes wide as saucers, with both hands clamped over her mouth.

In front of Trevor, Janice hadn't moved. But every thought was expressed clearly on her face. Her eyes were narrowed into little slits, her eyebrows were all scrunched in the middle, and her lips were pressed together so hard some of the skin around her mouth had turned white.

Then her foot started tapping. Behind him, he heard the bang as the ball came in contact with the pins.

"That's how you bowl. Like a girl," he said.

"Then you should bowl like a girl more often, because if this would have been your first ball, you would have just gotten a strike. Smarty-pants."

"Really? Are you kidding me?"

Her stone-faced expression told him she definitely wasn't in the mood to kid.

He spun around to face the pins once more, and sure enough, not one remained standing.

Trevor grinned from ear to ear as he turned back to Janice. "Hey. I got a strike. How about that?"

"I said, if it was your *first* ball it would have been a strike. That makes it a spare."

"Still. That was pretty good, don't you think?"

"That was horrible. How could you embarrass me like that?"

Trevor crossed his arms, matching her stance. He smirked. "Sorry, Darlin', but you do just fine at embarrassing yourself without me."

"I don't look nearly as stupid as you did."

"That's 'cause you're a girl. When girls do stuff like that, most guys think it's cute. If I did that, which I did, I just look ridiculous."

She didn't answer. She only continued to glare at him.

As the silence drew on, Trevor realized that Frank and Laura were watching them, as were the people in the lanes on either side of theirs. The longer they continued to stand there, the more he realized that he really had embarrassed her, maybe not by imitating her, but by arguing with her about it where everyone could see.

Trevor stepped forward and raised one hand to touch her shoulder so he could usher her to a more private setting. Since it was the first time they were standing so close together since they arrived, Trevor hadn't realized how far down he had to look at her. Wearing the flat-soled bowling shoes, she was shorter than ever.

Before he could guide her away gently to a less public location, she flinched away from his hand and glared at him even more intently.

"Don't touch me," she hissed between her teeth. She spun around so fast her hair flopped. Without breaking the flow of the movement, Janice stomped off to the bench and plunked herself down beside Laura.

He grinned weakly at Frank and Laura, who were both staring at him. "I think she's mad at me," he mumbled as he passed them and sat beside Janice. He saw Laura whisper something in Frank's ear.

Trevor cleared his throat and sat as close to Janice as he could without her shuffling away. "I don't know what you're so mad about. I really don't like bowling, and I was getting frustrated. Maybe I did get a little carried away, but it was me who everyone was staring at, not you."

"It's not that everyone was staring at you. You were imitating me. Is that really what you think of me? I look that stupid when I bowl? And even if I do look that dumb, it wasn't very nice of you to make fun of me."

Laura leaned forward and glanced nervously between the two of them. "It's okay, Janice. You don't really look like that when you bowl. Trevor was totally overdoing it."

Frank stepped in front of Janice. "Yeah, Janice. He's just jealous 'cause everybody else bowls better than he does. Come on, give him a break. He didn't mean to hurt your feelings. Did you, Trev?"

Judging from her expression, she was more angry than hurt, but he supposed there was some of that too. "Would it help if I said I was sorry?"

Janice heaved a sigh. "I don't know why I'm so angry. That's okay, Trevor. I probably do look a little silly when I bowl. Other people have teased me about it, but no one has ever done such an active demonstration. I guess that's why it kind of hit me between the eyes. Now let's finish up this game and get out of here. The leagues are going to be starting soon, and we don't have much time left."

Laura rose and selected a ball to take her turn.

While Janice watched Laura, Trevor watched Janice out the corner of his eye.

He'd made her angry again, with the same result as the last time. Everything blew up on the surface quickly, they settled it, and the disagreement was over within minutes.

Also the same as the last time, he'd crossed some kind of line he didn't know existed. He'd hurt her feelings, but instead of making him guess what he did wrong, she let him have it, holding nothing back. She did nothing to manipulate him by piling guilt on his head for hurting her feelings, and she didn't test him with guessing games. She didn't appear to be holding a grudge. He didn't need to make it up to her. There were no tears. They dealt with it. It was over.

The incident was both forgiven and forgotten by Janice, but Trevor wasn't going to soon forget. He'd never seen a woman handle hurt feelings like that before. He'd seen his sisters hold a grudge for weeks. Their boyfriends, and later their husbands, often went through extreme measures in order to make things right. Only when enough time had passed and proper restitution accomplished could the incident be sufficiently laid to rest. Like most men, he couldn't handle a woman's tears. He'd had girlfriends do the same to him, particularly Brenda. He'd seen it so often, in varying degrees, he thought it was normal.

Having a spat with Janice was almost like having an argument with Frank. Except, for some reason, when he fought with Janice he felt like doing something special for her to make up for it when it was over—not because he had to, but some deep little inner voice made him want to.

Janice rose as Laura approached the bench. "Good going, Laura. You're getting better already. I wish we had time for another game."

Trevor harrumphed under his breath. "Yeah, what a crying shame that we have to go. I just love bowling so much," he grumbled sarcastically.

Janice turned, scowled at him, turned back to Laura, smiled once again, and walked away to select her ball.

This time, when Janice wound up and did her walk up the approach area, her motions lacked the fluidity of her prior efforts. Trevor tried to convince himself that it was only his imagination that she didn't score as well as she had in previous rounds. Yet, she only smiled politely after her second throw and returned to her seat.

Frank rose for his turn, so Trevor shuffled closer to Janice. "You're pretty good."

"Not really. But I'm better than you." She closed her eyes, turned, and briefly stuck her tongue out at him, then turned back in time to watch Frank bowl a strike, allowing him to have another throw on their last turn.

"Yay, Frank!" Janice called.

Laura simply clapped her hands.

Trevor didn't care about Frank's score. He only cared that the bonus throw gave him a minute longer to sit with Janice.

"Are we going to do something else after this?"

She glanced at her watch, then spoke with her face turned straight ahead, watching Frank. "I don't think so. There really isn't time to do anything. We have to get up for work in the morning."

He sat in silence while Frank threw his last ball.

"Okay, Trevor, it's your turn," she said, still not looking at him as she spoke.

He wanted her to turn to him, with her eyes open this time. He wanted to see if those little green flecks were still there once she'd calmed down.

"Do I have to?"

"Yup." She nodded but didn't turn her head.

He leaned closer. "I think I'll forfeit my turn. I've got the lowest score anyway, so who cares?"

Suddenly, she did turn to him. Through her lenses, he could see the flecks were still there. When she realized how close his face was to hers, she tilted her head back as she spoke. "Quit being such a coward. Just because the whole place was watching your sterling performance last time and will be watching you again this time, you don't have to be nervous. You can bowl like a man now."

He couldn't hold back his laughter. "I had that coming, didn't I?"

She smiled. Something strange happened in his stomach, making him wonder if he was getting hungry.

"Yes, you did. Now get up there."

He continued to snicker to himself as he wound up and took his turn. He didn't bowl a strike or a spare, but he scored better than he had the entire game.

As he changed spots with Laura so she could take the last turn of the night, Laura whispered to him. "Good going, Trev, but I still beat you."

He grinned. "Ask me if I care."

While they returned the rented shoes, Trevor struggled to keep quiet and not comment about size of the shoes Janice laid on the counter. Next to his size twelve shoes, hers looked like a child's. Since he already knew that she was touchy about her height, or rather the lack thereof, he didn't want to take the risk that her sensitivity extended to her shoe size. He also didn't know why in the world he would find her shoe size so fascinating.

He didn't mind the distraction when Frank slapped him on the back. "Hey, Loser. How's it feel?"

"I really don't care. If nothing else, tonight was a good reminder of why I hate bowling."

Laura linked her hands through the crook in Frank's elbow. "I know what you mean. I don't exactly hate bowling, but I don't think this is going to become a favorite weekly thing for me either." Laura turned to Janice. "I don't feel like going home yet. How about if we go next door and grab a donut or something?" Laura then released Frank, leaned closer to Janice, and whispered something in her ear.

Trevor turned to watch Janice. Her cheeks darkened, she shook her head, and she suddenly stared at the floor. Something strange happened in his stomach again. Now he knew he had to be hungry.

He pasted a smile on his face. "Yeah. A donut sounds good. I've got to do something to make me forget about bowling."

The donut shop was considerably quieter than the bowling

alley. First, Janice slid into the booth. He prepared to slide in beside her, but Frank pointed at something out the window. Trevor couldn't see whatever interested Frank so much, and when he turned back around, Frank had already lost interest and taken the seat beside Janice. Laura slid into the other side of the booth, then patted the vinyl seat beside her, encouraging Trevor to sit beside her in what should have been Frank's spot.

Trevor shrugged his shoulders. Rather than make an issue of their strange behavior, he slid in beside Laura.

Now that they finally could begin with the issue at hand, he waited for Janice to start the conversation. However, Frank began monopolizing her attention, talking in hushed tones, not giving her the chance to speak to the group as a whole.

He felt Laura poking him in the ribs. She spoke in hushed tones as she leaned closer to him. "Trevor? If you ever need help with Janice, you can ask me anything. Did you know that her favorite color is purple?"

He blinked, rested one elbow on the table, and rested his cheek on his fist. "Really? Do you know what Frank's favorite color is?"

"It doesn't matter about Frank's favorite color. We have to talk about Janice."

"I think I can handle Janice just fine. Why don't we talk about Frank?"

Laura shook her head. His peripheral vision caught Janice shaking her head at Frank at the same time. Trevor thought it was kind of funny.

"No, we have to talk about Janice. She may have a few little quirks, but she's got a heart of gold."

Trevor struggled to keep a straight face. "Quirks? Janice? No. I hadn't noticed."

Laura nodded so fast her hair bounced. "It's true, and I only mean that in the kindest way. We've been best friends since elementary school, and I'd do anything for her." Laura's voice lowered in volume even more, forcing Trevor to lean closer to her in order to hear. "For starters, I warn you not to get her talking about junk food. Not that she's a health food nut—but she's very careful about what she eats."

He recalled Janice's comments on their lunch choices earlier in the day. Now he felt more than ever that he'd made a good decision in changing his selection from the greasy burger to the healthier submarine sandwich. "No kidding?" he asked, trying to keep the sarcasm from his voice.

Realizing he was fighting a losing battle, especially since Frank seemed to have Janice's attention completely tied up, Trevor listened politely to Laura as she told him everything about Janice and her likes and dislikes. The more he listened, the more he realized that Janice had been right. Laura should have known all Frank's likes and dislikes the way she knew Janice's. He wanted to point out to her that since Laura felt it very important that he knew all about Janice, then she should know the same about Frank. However, Laura didn't allow him the opportunity to change the subject.

The second Laura finished her donut, she cleared her throat. Trevor wondered if this had been a prearranged signal because Frank instantly pushed his coffee cup aside and stood. "Sorry, guys. I just noticed the time. Laura's got to be up at six. We should go."

Before he knew it, Trevor was in the passenger seat of Frank's car, and they were on their way home.

He only hoped Janice's efforts had obtained better results.

seven

"Janice, while you were gone for lunch, someone called for you. It sounded important. It was. . ." Susan picked up the yellow note. "Mr. T. Halliday. He's some kind of engineer at V. L. Management."

Janice stuffed the bag and her purse under her desk while she mumbled her thank-you to Susan for relieving her.

The second Susan disappeared around the corner, Janice dialed the number.

He answered in one ring. "Maintenance."

"It's me—Janice. What do you want, Trevor?"

The echoing drone of traffic in the distance drifted through the phone along with his voice. "There's going to be a slight change of plans tonight. I hope you don't mind."

Janice glanced down at the corner of the bag peeking out from beneath the desk. She'd spent her entire lunch break shopping for the coming evening. She could probably say she hated shopping as much as Trevor hated bowling.

She sighed. "No, I don't mind. What's the matter?"

Trevor didn't speak while the wail of a siren blasted in her ear through the handset. "Frank's got to work late tonight. Would you mind if you and Laura came here and picked us up instead of us picking you two up? That will give Frank the time he needs to shower and clean up before we all go out for dinner tonight at a decent time."

Another siren wailed through the phone. Janice waited until it passed before she spoke. "That's fine. I guess Laura's got your address?"

"Believe it or not, she's never been here. I'd better give it to you. You can't miss the mailbox in front. It's one of those red antique kinds on a post."

As she scribbled the address and made a note about the mailbox, another siren wailed.

"Where are you?" she asked after it passed. By the number, she knew he was on a cell phone. Not only did he seem to be outside, it sounded like he was in the middle of a busy intersection.

"I'm on the roof of one of the buildings removing a bird's nest from an air-conditioning intake duct. I'm having an easy day today. But judging from the fire trucks that just went by, I'm going to have a bad day tomorrow. But so far no ambulance, so that's a good thing."

She didn't want to think about cleaning up and rebuilding in the aftermath of a fire. Suddenly, she became more satisfied with her uneventful desk job. However, the thought of spending part of a workday up on the roof of a tall building did hold a certain amount of appeal. She wondered how much of the city he could see from his present perspective and if he ever took his camera with him.

Janice pictured a vivid pink and purple sunset from the vantage point of the roof of a tall building in a quiet section of town, businesses closing as people went home for the night. At nightfall, the glowing colors would be striking, but fading quickly. The evening air would blow a cool, refreshing breeze. The lights of the city would be slowly blinking on, just like a scene from an old romantic movie. . .a young couple in love, sharing a rare, quiet time together, hidden from the hustle and bustle of a long and hectic day, alone on the roof. . . .

Janice shook her head and cleared her throat, sending her foolish thoughts from her head. "So you want us at your place at six, then?"

"Six would work with our reservations. See you then."

"Okay. Oh, Trevor?"

"Yes?"

She opened her mouth but snapped it shut. "Nothing. See you at six," she said, then mumbled a quick good-bye and hung up.

Janice stared blankly at the door. She'd almost asked him if he was going to wear the same thing he'd worn to church on Sunday. Only this time she wouldn't have asked him to take off the suit jacket or the tie.

Janice buried her face in her hands. She didn't want to know what Trevor was going to wear.

Now she only had to convince herself that she didn't care.

※

Laura knocked on Trevor and Frank's front door, then turned around and called to her down the length of the sidewalk. "Come on, Janice. You look fine."

"I'll be there in a sec," Janice muttered around the key fob she held between her teeth. Somehow, the elastic waistband of her slip had become twisted, and when she slid out of the car, the left side of the slip slid up and became entangled at the waistband beneath her dress. Now the wretched garment wouldn't go down without a little convincing.

She tried to position herself discreetly, standing in the vee between the open car door and the car itself while she tried to grip the slip and pull it down through the fabric of her skirt.

If she had been in a more private setting, she could have simply reached under her skirt and yanked it down. However, not only was she on public display in the middle of Trevor and Frank's neighborhood, but soon Trevor would see her.

This was one of the reasons she hated wearing a dress.

Finally, she managed to tug it down properly into position, so it now lay flat beneath the skirt. Quickly, she swiped her hand down the front of herself to smooth a wrinkle that had appeared from being scrunched up while driving and made her way to Trevor's front door.

Her ankles wobbled as she tried to maintain her balance in the high heels while hurrying up the sidewalk. She felt more comfortable, and safer, in her sneakers.

This was another reason she hated wearing a dress.

Trevor opened the door just as her foot reached the first of the three steps leading to the porch.

He smiled when he saw Laura, but when he looked at Janice, his eyes widened, his smile dropped, and his mouth literally fell open.

Janice could almost feel his gaze as he scanned her from head to foot and then back to her face.

Her face flamed. While she wasn't fat, she'd never been thin, especially compared to Laura. All her life she'd been cursed with a flat chest, a big rear end, and chunky thighs, something the fitted waist of her dress only accented.

Another reason she hated dresses.

Trevor cleared his throat and reached up to fumble with the knot of his tie.

Janice's heart stopped beating for a second. He really was wearing the tie. And a different suit jacket. With matching pants. He'd also recently shaved.

"Wow. . . ," he mumbled, his voice trailing off.

Laura shrugged her shoulders and walked past him while Trevor stepped forward. He stood at the top step and extended his hand toward her to help Janice up the few steps.

Janice couldn't move her feet. All she could do was stare up at him.

"I'll go right in," Laura said, already inside the front door.

Not really wanting to, but not wanting to embarrass herself any further, Janice decided to throw dignity and decorum out the window. She grabbed the sides of her skirt at midthigh with both hands, hiked it up a couple of inches to allow her sufficient leeway to move her legs, and put one foot on the first step.

Obviously, women's clothes were designed by men who never considered that sometimes a woman would have to walk up stairs.

Another reason she hated wearing a dress.

Trevor broke out into a wide smile. Little crinkles appeared at the corners of his shining blue eyes. "This is a—"

Laura's scream pierced the air.

Trevor spun and ran into the living room. Janice hiked her

skirt up even more and ran behind him, doing her best not to stumble in the ridiculous shoes.

"What is that?!" Laura shrieked, pointing to a five-foot-wide aquarium set prominently against the living room wall.

Janice studied the aquarium. Instead of water and brightly colored fishes, gravel lined the bottom of the unit. The whole aquarium floor was scattered with rocks and sticks and numerous tropical plants.

She stepped closer. In the corner, one of the rocks was a strange color, not gray, but markedly brown and tan—with distinct geometric lines differentiating the color variations and patterns.

And then the rock moved.

Janice stepped closer. It wasn't a rock at all. The "rock" was merely a length folded in half, both halves extending along in a flowing line down the side of the aquarium and then along the back.

"It's a snake," she said. "And it's big."

Trevor stepped beside her. "This is Freddie, Frank's Burmese python."

Laura didn't move. She stood at a safe distance from the snake, her eyes wide, both hands pressed to her heart, and her purse on the floor, its contents scattered at her feet.

"It's ugly," Janice said softly. "Why would anyone want such a thing?"

"Frank's had it since he was a kid. It wasn't nearly this size when he got it, oh, about twelve or thirteen years ago. When he moved out—strange thing—his mother told him she didn't want Freddie in the house any longer, so he had to take Freddie with him. Imagine that, huh?"

Janice stepped up to the aquarium, steadied herself by touching her palms to the glass, and then bent at the waist to see the snake better. With her nose nearly touching the aquarium side, she studied the monstrous creature. "How long is that thing?"

Trevor hunkered down, squatting beside her near the

aquarium. "I guess it's about nine feet. Maybe ten."

"I don't think I want to know what Frank feeds it."

"Nope. You don't."

"That's what I thought."

Before she had a chance to ask about average life expectancy and molting patterns, Frank's voice sounded from behind them.

"Sorry about this. I don't usually have to work late on Tuesdays. Are we all ready to go?" Frank paused for a couple of seconds. His voice dropped to a low whisper. "Who is that?" he asked, directing his question at Laura, who remained a healthy distance from the snake habitat.

Janice squeezed her eyes shut. Of course Frank couldn't recognize her. Not only had he never seen her in a dress in the whole two years she'd known him, she was bent over studying his snake. All he could see of her was her too-wide behind sticking in the air.

She stood and turned around slowly.

"Janice? You look great! Doesn't she look great, Trev? Did you tell her she looks great?"

Trevor stood as well, and Janice noticed that his cheeks had darkened. She seldom saw a man blush, and she thought it quite endearing.

"Uh, no, I didn't. But I meant to."

Janice felt her own cheeks darken as well. "You guys both look good too." Especially Trevor, who was taller and not as stocky as Frank. Frank's hair was still slightly damp from the shower. He also wore a sport coat like Trevor, but Frank's top button on his shirt was unfastened, and he wasn't wearing a tie.

Trevor checked his watch. "We should be leaving in a couple of minutes. Are you nearly done, Frank?"

Frank ran his fingers through his hair, then glanced at Trevor. "Do I need a tie? Give me another minute, and I'll be right there. I'll meet you at the car."

Janice allowed Trevor to escort her outside and down the steps while Laura waited inside for Frank.

"We have to talk," she said as they neared the car.

"You've got that right," Trevor mumbled.

At the same time, they both glanced toward the house, confirming Frank and Laura both remained inside.

"By the way," he said, "you really do look nice. I thought you told me yesterday that you don't own a blue dress."

"I went out and bought it on my lunch break," she said, once more turning her face to the front door. She still couldn't believe that she'd bought a new dress, never mind that she was actually wearing it. Most of all, she couldn't figure out whatever had possessed her to do such a thing for a single occasion. "But never mind this dumb dress. We've got to discuss what we're going to do tonight. Last night was a disaster."

Trevor nodded. "I know. Laura didn't give me a chance to talk to her about Frank because she was too busy giving me a list of all your good and bad points. Just like what you said we should do for them. I couldn't get a word in."

Janice felt her face flame. She deliberately focused far too much attention on inserting the key into the door lock. "Frank did the same about you. Laura's also been bugging me, asking if you and I have kissed and made up yet. Tonight, we've got to get them talking about themselves and each other. If the conversation starts to drift, point it back to the wedding to get them back on track."

He nodded again. "I agree." Once more, he checked his watch and glanced toward the house. "They still haven't come out. Maybe we're worrying for nothing while they're fighting about Freddie, and the wedding is off. Did you see her face?"

"Yes. I thought she'd seen a ghost or something. You have to admit that a snake isn't exactly a normal pet."

He continued to watch the front door. "I know. I'm a dog person, myself. One day, when I get married, I'm going to get a nice, fuzzy, ugly-type mutt. Maybe I'll rescue a dog that's going to be put down at the animal shelter. I've always wanted to do that. I think mutts make great pets. Especially for kids."

Janice nodded as she secured her purse strap more firmly over her shoulder. "Me too. Here they come. Oh dear. They're holding hands. It looks like Laura recovered from her fear of snakes."

Trevor sighed. "I guess that would have been too easy. Here goes nothing."

Since it was her car, Janice drove to the restaurant, which ended up being much more luxurious than she had anticipated.

Instead of durable, industrial-type carpet or tile, the lobby floor was constructed of rich, dark hardwood flooring. Muted shades of pale green and dark burgundy served as the main colors of the decor, blending with assorted hand-painted pictures of both meadow and mountain scenery framed with dark antique wood the same color as the flooring. Fine lace curtains covered the windows, allowing some light to enter the room while providing a barrier from the outside world. Strains of classical music echoed in the background, loud enough to be pleasant, but soft enough to allow quiet, private conversations at each table. A flickering candle graced each table, and a single, low-wattage overhead lamp cast a soft glow on the patrons' faces and just enough light to read the menu, giving each table a distinctly intimate atmosphere.

The servers and the hostess were clothed in black slacks or skirts, black shoes, and starched, pleated white shirts adorned by a black bow tie, completing the elegant mood of the establishment.

While Trevor gave his name to the hostess, another couple entered, also dressed to the nines, making Janice suddenly grateful for her impulsive decision to purchase the blue dress for the occasion.

The hostess smiled and led their group to their reserved table. Frank and Laura followed first, and Janice lagged behind. She slowed her pace, then poked Trevor in the ribs to get his attention so he would walk slower with her to create a space between them and Laura and Frank, allowing her to speak candidly.

"Look at this place," she ground out in a stage whisper. "How much is this going to cost?"

He bent toward her as they walked. "None of your business," he replied. "Frank and I already discussed it, and we're paying. Don't even think about it. It's our treat. Besides, this is supposed to be a date. You're supposed to smile pretty while we all make nice to each other at the table."

"Don't worry. I'm not going to wreck the evening arguing about money. We can deal with that later. The point is that we're supposed to be getting them to assess their relationship realistically. This place is too. . ." She struggled to find the right word. "Romantic!"

He turned toward her for a brief second, not altering his pace. "Shh. Trust me."

Strangely, she did.

The hostess seated them at a table by a large window overlooking a small pond full of lily pads and a flock of ducks happily floating about.

True to his word, Trevor did manage to steer the conversation toward points of mutual interest, as well as conflicting interests, without allowing the discussions to become dissonant. Janice thought that if it were herself instead of Laura, she would definitely have started to have doubts about her compatibility, or incompatibility, with Frank over the long-term by now.

However, Laura wasn't Janice. Laura just didn't get the message. Nothing she or Trevor said seemed to make a difference.

Instead of getting even more frustrated with Laura's inability to see the situation realistically, Janice changed her focus to trying to figure out why Laura was so intent on marrying Frank, a man with whom she had little or nothing in common.

Janice had met Laura in elementary school, and they'd been inseparable since. Laura was intelligent and exercised good judgment, except for the current situation, and showed a promising career as a design consultant. At the same time, Laura also had an interest in children, and Janice knew that

Laura intended to put her career aside for a few years to raise a family.

Laura's hobbies and interests also revolved around her creative bent. She enjoyed crafts and making things. Laura sewed much of her own clothing—but not because it was less expensive to sew a garment with the high cost of the designer fabrics she selected. Laura sewed because she loved the process of creating something with her own hands. Laura also enjoyed cooking. However, neither of them enjoyed cleaning. Still, when their home was a mess, it bothered Laura much more than it bothered Janice.

In many ways, they were like a female version of the Odd Couple. In the same way as Laura and Frank, many of Janice and Laura's likes and dislikes were opposite. However, their differences were complementary opposites, not opposites that would drive each other nuts in the long run. Besides, Janice only lived with Laura. She wasn't married to her. They both knew their arrangement of sharing the house was only as permanent as the first one of them getting married and leaving.

The relationship Laura planned with Frank was for keeps. Therefore, there had to be a different set of rules.

Even though she didn't know Frank that well, Janice knew him well enough. Now, as Trevor did his best to point out the differences between Frank and Laura, she knew more than ever that Frank and Laura were not suited for each other.

The night progressed pleasantly due to Trevor's quick wit and persistent patience. The more they talked, the less Janice could understand what Laura saw in Frank as a marriage partner. Neither did she see what Frank saw in Laura.

Despite Trevor's efforts, nothing changed. Janice could tell the minute he gave up for the evening. He turned the subject to a topic totally unrelated to relationships or anything anyone was specifically interested in, and they simply enjoyed the rest of the evening as four friends out together.

The drive home turned out to be equally pleasant and uneventful.

When Janice stopped in front of Frank and Trevor's house, her mind went blank. Officially, the evening had been a date. She'd never driven a man home after a date; she had always been the passenger. At the end of the date, he would walk her to the door. Depending on how well they knew each other, how long they had been seeing each other, and how much she liked him, the night would end with a peck on the cheek or a short, chaste kiss at the front door.

Since she was the one dropping Trevor off, Janice didn't know if she was supposed to escort him to the door or if he was simply supposed to leave her at the car and go into his house alone. Either way, she didn't know if she was supposed to kiss him good night or if he was supposed to kiss her good night. She wondered if she could get away with simply shaking hands and going their separate ways.

Frank and Laura exited the car and walked to the door, leaving her alone with Trevor, making her more uncertain than ever. Even though she'd been alone with him before, that had been at lunchtime, in the middle of the day, in the middle of downtown. This time, they were parked on a dark street, and they'd just been on an official date. As they now sat, it would have been a simple matter for him to lean toward her and kiss her good night.

Janice cleared the car so fast she didn't know how she didn't slam her skirt in the door. She praised God for the small miracle that her slip didn't ride up under her dress this time.

Trevor exited the car slowly and began walking around to her side. She glanced at the porch where Frank and Laura were standing, facing each other, talking quietly, their hands clasped between them. She couldn't interrupt Frank and Laura, but she had no place else to go, so she remained beside the driver's door of her car.

By the time Trevor arrived beside her, she couldn't stop her knees from trembling.

He stood so close to her, their toes almost touched.

He shrugged his shoulders. "I tried, but this didn't exactly go as I'd hoped."

"I know."

Trevor glanced at Frank and Laura, who hadn't moved from their spot on the porch. "I think we'll have to try another double date. Next time, I'll have to approach things differently, though."

Janice nodded. "I agree."

He continued to look into her face. One eyebrow quirked up.

"Frank is really concerned that you're still mad at me. You're not still mad, are you?"

She shook her head. No words came out.

He smiled. "Good."

Even in the indirect light from the streetlamp, she could see those adorable little crinkles forming at the corners of his eyes. Blue eyes. At least, normally they were blue. In the muted light, she could only see a slim ring of the light blue around his pupils. Standing so close, she had to tip her head up to see better.

Before she realized what he was doing, Trevor lowered his head slightly. Slowly, both hands came up, and his palms cupped her chin. "I know it wasn't a real date, but I had a really nice time. Thank you."

As she continued to stare up into Trevor's eyes, they drifted shut. He lowered his head.

He was going to kiss her.

She was too stunned to move away.

With the utmost gentleness, his warm lips covered hers.

She couldn't help it. She closed her eyes too.

And then the kiss was over, or at least she thought it was over. However, instead of pulling away completely, he tilted his head, and his mouth found hers again, this time the contact slightly firmer.

She lifted her hands to his chest, meaning to push him away if he tried anything more than a simple kiss, but the feeling of his heart pounding beneath her palms stopped her. Instead of wanting him to stop, the warmth of his chest beneath her hands and her awareness that his heartbeat had quickened only made his kiss sweeter.

Suddenly, his mouth left hers. He released her chin and stepped back. With the loss, despite the warm spring evening air, she felt strangely cold.

He backed up exactly one step. "Good night, Janice," he said, his voice lower pitched than usual, and oddly rough sounding.

"Good night, Trevor," she mumbled back.

In the still of the night, the soles of Trevor's leather shoes tapped as he walked up the concrete sidewalk. Laura walked down the three steps of the porch at the same time as Trevor walked up.

Janice hustled back into the car and drove off the second Laura closed the door. Laura stared out the window in silence for the entire drive home, which was fine with Janice.

She didn't know what had just happened with Trevor, but one thing she did know.

It would never happen again.

eight

Trevor knocked on Janice and Laura's door and waited.

Once again, he glanced to the street, noting the absence of Janice's car, which was not a bad thing. Part of him wanted to see her, but part of him wanted to run for the hills.

He still couldn't figure out why he'd kissed her. It hadn't even been a real date, and they both knew it. Still, when she looked up at him like that, he couldn't not kiss her. One little peck hadn't been enough, either. He'd gone and kissed her twice.

Not that she had acted any different than usual, but Trevor wondered if she realized how attractive she was in that dress—not in the sense of a model's perfect features kind of beauty, nor was she as pretty as Laura, at least on the outside. Janice's beauty lay in the richness of her smile and the sparkle in her eyes behind her glasses. At first he'd scoffed at her "what you see is what you get" statement, but the more he came to know her, the more he appreciated it. What Laura had called a quirk made Janice more attractive than any woman he'd ever dated for real.

Because of the quasi-date status of the evening, in the back of his mind he'd kept trying to figure out if she'd gone out and bought that special dress just for him. He knew that he'd chosen his own clothes very carefully last night, not just because they were going to a fancy place. He'd dressed extra special for Janice.

When she'd shown up in that dress, it had thrown him for a loop. He'd been so rattled that he'd missed telling her how pretty she looked before Frank dragged it out of him. The omission bothered him.

To top it off, his last words before they parted echoed in his head. He squeezed his eyes shut and sucked in a deep breath.

90

"I had a really nice time," he'd said. He couldn't believe how lame that sounded. He should have told her he'd had fun, but they'd only gone out for dinner, and "fun" was the wrong word too.

He could have said the evening had been enjoyable, but that felt too stuffy. He didn't know what the evening had been, but "nice" certainly wasn't the right word.

The sound of the door opening drew his thoughts back to where they should have been in the first place.

"Trevor?" Laura tipped her head to one side to look behind him. "What are you doing here?"

"Frank didn't come with me. He had to work late. I found this on the floor." He paused and held up a pink address book. "I knew it had to belong to either you or Janice because it sure doesn't belong to me or Frank."

"That's mine. It must have fallen out of my purse when I saw that horrible snake," she mumbled. "Come on in. Janice should be home in a few minutes."

Trevor glanced behind him to the street, confirming that Janice's little red car really wasn't approaching quite yet. "Sorry, I really should be going. Everyone has to get up early in the morning."

He started to turn around, but Laura grabbed him by the wrist. "Nonsense. You can stay for a couple of minutes. I'm sure she'd be disappointed if she knew she missed you. She should be home any minute."

Trevor wasn't as sure as Laura, but he didn't want to look like a coward and run since Laura had already pulled him inside and closed the front door.

"You want some tea? It's made."

"No, thanks. I'm a coffee person."

Laura shrugged her shoulders. "Suit yourself. If you don't mind, I'm going to refill my cup. I'll be right back."

With that, she disappeared into the kitchen, leaving Trevor alone in the living room.

Prior to his arrival, he hadn't thought about the possibility of being alone with Laura. He had simply planned to return the address book and leave. He hadn't thought about the opportunity the situation provided to do what he had missed doing on the weekend, which was to talk to Laura privately.

As he sat thinking of what to say, the doorknob rattled, the door opened, and Janice walked in. Despite the dry weather, her T-shirt appeared damp. If he didn't know any better, and if she were a guy, he would have thought he saw sweat stains extending from beneath her armpits. Besides the dingy T-shirt, her jeans were ratty and had a hole in one knee. Her hair hung limply in clumps, and even from across the room, he could see a big fingerprint smear on one of her lenses.

"Trevor? What are you doing here?"

He tried not to let his mouth gape open. If she hadn't been so calm and collected, he would have asked if something was wrong. If nothing were wrong, his next question would have been how she could be out in public like that. As she was now, Trevor could barely believe that the untidy person before him was the same delicate woman he'd so gently kissed last night.

Not wanting to say or do the wrong thing, Trevor chose to say nothing about her appearance. He leaned back on the couch and crossed his arms over his chest. "When I got home from work, I found an address book on the floor. I knew it had to belong to one of you, so I brought it over, and Laura asked me to stay. She said you would be mad at me if I left without seeing you. I don't ever want to make you mad."

"Very funny." Janice kicked off her sneakers, wiggled her toes, and walked into the room but didn't sit down. "Okay, you've seen me. Now you can go."

Instead of leaving, he stretched out his legs and crossed his ankles. It was killing him. He couldn't help it. He had to ask. "Where were you? You look like you've just crawled out from beneath a rock."

Her lower lip protruded over her top lip and she blew out a puff of air to blow her hair out of her face. When that didn't work, she reached up and swiped her hair back with her hand.

He didn't want to notice, but now he was positive she really did have sweat stains under her arms.

"I was at my exercise class. I go once a week and most Saturdays. Once a month we wear street clothes instead of our regular uniform so we can get used to the restricted movement."

Trevor blinked. "Uniform? I knew women wore those spandex thingies, but I didn't know they were called uniforms."

"It's really a women's self-defense class."

Trevor blinked. "And you need a uniform for that?"

For the first time, he noticed what was on her T-shirt. It pictured a woman wearing a martial arts uniform, one leg extended at waist height and her fists close to her body beneath her long, flowing hair. Below the picture, in bold, black letters were the words "Yes, I really do kick like a girl."

Trevor stood. He took one step toward Janice, but she raised her palms in the air toward him. "I warn you. Come near me at your own risk. I stink." She wiggled her toes inside her socks again to further emphasize the point. Her words "what you see is what you get" once more echoed in his head.

He grinned and approached her anyway, appraising the size of her. For the moment, since Janice was shoeless, he now stood a full foot taller than she did, maybe more. She was so short, he wondered if her legs were much longer than his arms. He couldn't see her successfully defending herself against anyone older than twelve, and even that was doubtful.

He couldn't hold back a snicker. "You say you stink, but I think you need more for self-defense than body odor."

Her eyes narrowed. Suddenly, Trevor knew he'd crossed that line again.

"It's a martial arts class, and I have my red belt. If we weren't in the middle of my living room, I could really hurt you. You're lucky that as a Christian, I abhor violence."

"Then why are you taking such a thing?"

Her eyes widened. Silence hung in the air for a long, few seconds. Laura, teacup in hand, walked into the room.

Janice's voice came out so soft he barely heard her. "Because I work downtown," she squeaked. Without elaborating further, she turned and ran out of the room before he could say a word.

Something in Trevor's gut clenched. He had a bad feeling there was more to the story than simply the location of her workplace. The possibility that she'd once been attacked on a downtown street being the reason she would take martial arts for self-defense nearly made him sick. She could have been really hurt. . .or worse. He felt even sicker knowing he'd teased her about it.

"Janice! Wait!" he called out, totally ignoring Laura. He ran to the entrance of the hallway and stopped, not knowing if he should go farther. Janice hadn't exactly invited him in—Laura had. Actually, now that he thought about it, Janice had specifically told him to leave.

A door down the hall slammed shut, making his decision for him. "I don't care that you stink!" he called out louder. "We need to talk!"

"Blew it again, huh, lover boy?" Laura muttered behind him, sipping her tea as she spoke.

Trevor sighed. "Apparently," he mumbled.

She sat on the couch, rested her cup on top of a magazine on the coffee table, and picked up a church bulletin that was on the arm of the couch. She opened it, and one finger trailed down the right side. "Janice thinks that Frank and I should take this couples' course our pastor is running. The little blurb says it's not just for couples who are about to be married. It's also for anyone who is considering getting engaged or even for someone who isn't necessarily thinking about getting married but wants to explore their current relationship. Frank and I talked about it, and we're not going to go, but maybe you and Janice should. You two really seem to need it. If you don't mind me saying so."

Trevor stared blankly at Laura while Laura reread the course outline. "It says it starts this week. It's on Friday nights, for twelve weeks."

Trevor turned his head and continued to stare blankly at the vacant hallway. He didn't need to take such a course. He and Janice weren't even dating for real. As soon as Laura and Frank split up, he would never see Janice again except when they bumped into each other with mutual friends, just as they always had.

For some reason, he didn't want that to happen. The thought of hardly ever seeing her again gave him a stab of loss in the pit of his gut.

He didn't want to date her, but he did want to be her friend.

A light bulb went on in his head.

He turned to Laura. "We'll go if you go."

Laura knotted her eyebrows and lowered the bulletin to her lap. "I beg your pardon?"

"I have three sisters who got married. Even though they're older than me, I could tell that when they took those premarital things, it was really good for their relationships. I'm not sure entirely what goes on, but all three of them said they got to know their future husbands much better and much faster than if they'd only been dating and hadn't taken the premarital sessions. These things are all about sharing and mutual needs and getting to know a person, really deep down, where it counts. I think it would be really great for you and Frank to go. That way, you could get to know each other really, really well. Before the wedding."

"I don't know. I don't think Frank would want to go. We planned to opt out for one single session where we would sit down with the pastor only once just before the wedding."

"I think Janice is right. Taking a twelve-week thing is a great idea. Besides, what's twelve short little weeks in the span of an entire lifetime?"

"I don't want to go if we won't know anyone else there."

Trevor grinned and struggled not to rub his hands together with glee. "You won't be alone. You guys will be with me and Janice."

Laura picked up the bulletin and read it to herself once more.

Trevor glanced again to the vacant looming entranceway to the hall, which led to the room Janice was now hiding in.

If the only way Frank and Laura would go to the couples' course was if he and Janice went, then that was the way it had to be. They both had failed in their quest for Frank and Laura to see each other in a realistic light. Janice had the right idea in trying to convince Frank and Laura to attend. It was time to call in the experts.

"I guess we'll go, then," Laura muttered, still reading. "But only if you guys go."

He wondered what Janice would say when she found out.

୨৯

"Good evening and welcome, everyone. Let's all introduce ourselves."

Janice said her name in turn as the introductions went around the big circle. Including themselves, eight couples were in attendance, and one more couple who couldn't make it tonight was scheduled to join the following week.

Pastor Harry smiled at everyone and folded his hands in his lap. "Before we start, I want each of you to hold the hand of the person you came with and look them in the eye as I say this." He paused while everyone in the room shuffled. A few of the young women giggled.

Trevor reached for her hand and gave it a gentle squeeze. He smiled and spoke softly, barely moving his lips. "It's okay. It's only twelve weeks."

She forced herself to smile back, knowing these were going to be the longest twelve weeks of her life.

Pastor Harry cleared his throat. "Now that you're looking at each other, I want you to listen carefully to what I'm saying. Everyone brings their good traits and their bad traits into a relationship. You are the person you are, just as the person with you is the person they are. This is the person you have fallen in love with. Look at them carefully. Most likely, they are not going to change very much as the years go by, just as you are not going to change that much either. Some of you have wedding plans in the near future, and some of you don't. But I think that you all recognize the possibility, and that's why you're here.

"If you think you are going to change your partner after the wedding, you're wrong. Tell yourself right now, it's not going to happen. One of the biggest mistakes people make when they get married is thinking that they're going to change their partner and make them into what they want their partner to be after the wedding.

"So if your partner drives you nuts with the remote control and never-ending channel flipping. . ."

A number of the ladies giggled.

"Or if it drives you bananas when your partner thinks they need five hundred pairs of shoes when one or two will do—"

"Hear, hear!" one of the men called out, followed by more giggling and a light smack on the man's knee.

"Then I'm afraid you'll have to get used to it because it's not going to change. Welcome to our Getting To Know You, Spring Session."

Janice leaned closer to Trevor. "Are you a channel flipper?" she asked softly.

Trevor tipped his head down so he could whisper in her ear. "No. How many pairs of shoes do you own?"

She grinned. Maybe, just maybe, this wouldn't be so bad after all. "Three if you count my sandals. Plus my sneakers and my boots."

Trevor grinned back. "I like you better already."

The pastor handed a booklet to each person.

"We're going to start out with this as an introduction. This centers on what you are willing to put into a relationship versus what you expect to get out of one. Above all, I want everyone to be honest, because you are fooling no one. This is for you and you alone and sometimes, for your partner. There are no right or wrong answers. I'm not going to ask anyone to share anything they don't feel comfortable talking about in a group. We'll have eleven group sessions, and for the last one,

I'll see every couple privately. If anyone feels they want to speak to me in a private appointment at any time, just ask. That's what I'm here for. Does everyone have a pen?"

Janice dug two pens out of her purse, one for herself and one for Trevor, and they started writing. She found she didn't know the answers to a lot of the questions because she didn't know Trevor well enough. In the back of her mind, she wondered how Laura and Frank were doing, which was the reason she was here in the first place.

She really and truly hoped they were doing better than she was. Her point was not to rub it in their faces that they didn't know enough about each other well enough to delve headfirst into a marriage relationship. Her goal was for them to discover more about each other, and along with the discoveries would come the realization that they were not suited to each other for the lifelong commitment of marriage.

When everyone present answered all the questions, they had an open session for discussion. Janice had nothing to contribute, but many people present did share their answers with the group. Listening gave Janice quite an insight on the development of interpersonal relationships with men in general. She decided to keep some of what she learned in a little file in her head for future use, for when she finally did meet the man who would be her Mr. Right.

At the close of the session, the pastor thanked everyone for coming, then encouraged all the couples to discuss their answers with each other, first to get to know each other better, and second, as a side benefit, for everyone to get to know themselves better. He invited everyone to stay for coffee and goodies, which were set out on a table in the lobby, so everyone in the group could continue to talk in the less structured atmosphere.

If things continued the way they were, Janice had a feeling that by the time the twelve weeks were over, they would all know each other a lot better, regardless of coffee and snack time, by the nature of the reason they were together.

Janice walked to the coffeemaker to help herself. While she poured her coffee, she quickly glanced over her shoulder at Trevor, who was standing near the doorway yakking with Frank and Laura, coffee and donut already in hand.

Specifically, she knew that she and Trevor would get to know each other much better through the material provided. So far, in the concentrated time they'd spent together before the course started today, she'd already come to know him much better. He wasn't at all what she expected.

She again thought about her first impression of him being the quiet type. Now, she definitely knew better. After he warmed up, he had a delightful sense of humor and a sharp wit, even if he did tend to go a little overboard. But then, if she had to look deep down inside herself, which this material Pastor Harry gave everyone was forcing her to do, she had to admit that she enjoyed egging him on. Since they'd started spending so much time together, she had to admit that she kind of liked Trevor, as a friend only, of course.

She lowered her head and smiled to herself, thinking of his response to her "I stink" comment. She would have completely lost all respect for him if he hadn't responded in kind. Of course he rose to the challenge, even if his response had been a bit insensitive. Still, she'd had it coming. She'd fully enjoyed the banter until he asked the one question that had sent her running to her bedroom like a scared rabbit. Now, a couple of days later, he thankfully hadn't brought the subject up. However, she feared this wasn't the end of it.

The whole purpose of the course was to get to know each other better, whether she wanted to or not. That being the case, she had no doubt that the subject matter would back her into a corner, and she'd have to tell him.

Maybe she could come down with a killer flu that night.

For now, she hoped that he would forget about it if she became less outspoken and behaved herself. She would miss the verbal banter, but it was now time to play the girlfriend role, which meant not doing what others might perceive as fighting, no matter how much fun they had doing it.

Later, when they no longer had to concentrate on the situation with Frank and Laura or what people thought, she could once again enjoy countering him in a battle of wits.

She hadn't realized how long she'd been standing still at the coffeemaker until one of the men whom she recognized from the Friday night young adult group appeared beside her.

"Hi, Janice."

"Hi, Dan. It's good to see you here. I heard that you and Allyson were recently engaged. Congratulations." This time, Janice found she meant it, unlike the last time she nearly choked on the same word.

A smile flitted across Dan's face. He quickly glanced down at her left hand, then at Trevor, who was still with Frank and Laura, along with another couple. "It's nice to see you here— quite a surprise." He jerked his head toward Trevor. "Sorry, I forgot your boyfriend's name; there are so many people here tonight. Seeing you here with another guy is a real surprise. I thought you were going out with Rick."

Janice quirked her eyebrows. She'd been with Rick in a group, but she'd never been out with him alone. "Rick? What makes you say that?"

Dan shrugged his shoulders. "Oh, just stuff I heard."

She opened her mouth to ask what he'd heard, but before she could get a word out, Trevor appeared beside her. She nearly spilled her freshly poured coffee when Trevor slipped his arm around her waist.

"Hi. . ." Trevor scanned Dan's name tag, then smiled at him. "Dan. Nice to meet you. I assume you already know Janice?"

"Yes. We were just talking about being here. I didn't know she was engaged."

Janice turned her head to gauge Trevor's response.

Trevor's smile widened, and his grip around her waist tightened. "Well, we're not officially engaged, at least not right now. But you never know, right?" He gave Dan an exaggerated wink.

Janice grabbed Trevor's hand at the same time as she forced a smile at Dan. "Excuse us, please. We have to talk."

Without waiting for Trevor or Dan to respond, she dragged Trevor away, holding firmly onto his wrist.

"Have you noticed we seem to need to do a lot of talking?" he asked as soon as she positioned him in a relatively private corner of the room.

Janice crossed her arms over her chest. "Just what did you think you were doing back there?"

"Did I do something wrong?"

"Didn't anyone ever tell you not to answer a question with a question?"

"Why do you ask?"

Janice dragged her hand over her face.

His goofy smile dropped. "Seriously, don't you think that since we're here, we should give people the impression that we're having a serious relationship? Face it. The few people who are here who aren't officially," he paused, making quotation marks in the air with his fingers for emphasis, "*engaged* are right on the verge of popping the question. They just want to tie up a few loose ends and answer a few questions first before they make the big decision. You know, the opposite of what Frank and Laura have done?"

Janice exhaled a long, deep sigh. "I suppose you're right. You just caught me off guard with your little performance. Have you ever gone to acting school?"

He puffed out his chest, pressed one palm, fingers splayed, over the center of his chest, and cleared his throat. "Hey. I'm a multitalented kind of guy."

After promising herself that she was going to be more demure and act the girlfriend role, Janice bit back the comment that was on the tip of her tongue. "Never mind," she grumbled as they started walking back to join their friends. "I guess you're right; that is what people are thinking. We'd better get back there before everybody thinks the wedding's off and we won't be coming back for the next fun-filled eleven weeks."

He nodded. "Oh, by the way, the four of us are going on another double date tomorrow night. Laura wants to go see that new chick flick with what's-his-face."

Janice's feet skidded to a halt, and she spun around, forcing Trevor to stop as well. "I know which one she's been wanting to see. I forget the name, but I heard it's bad. I hope you didn't say we would go."

"Uh. . .I've got some good news and some bad news."

She squeezed her eyes shut, sighed, then continued walking.

With any luck, all four cars would get flat tires and the buses would go on strike so they would have to walk to the video store and rent a good action movie instead.

nine

Trevor couldn't believe what he was seeing. He leaned back in the chair and folded his arms over his chest. "Aw, that's so fake. You can tell it's a backdrop. The same tree keeps reappearing as she's running in a supposedly straight line. See that leaf pattern over there? You'll see it again in a few seconds."

"Never mind that. I bet a log magically appears, and she's going to fall. Oh! Told you so!"

Suddenly Janice jumped in her chair. Trevor quickly glanced to the side to see Laura poking Janice in the ribs. "Will you two shut up?" Laura whispered roughly between her teeth. "You're ruining it!"

"Sorry," Trevor and Janice mumbled in unison.

Trevor leaned closer to Janice's ear. "I'm not really sorry. Are you?"

She giggled, and it was a lovely sound. "Nope. This movie isn't so bad after all. If you know what to watch for."

He leaned closer until his lips brushed her hair as he spoke. He could smell some kind of herbal shampoo. It suited her. "Bet she has a sprained ankle, and he has to help her run now."

She tilted her head more in his direction and turned so she now whispered in his ear. "Of course. Next he's going to fight the rabid wolf with his bare hands and win. Just wait and see."

Trevor shook his head. "No. She can't appear too weak. She'll stand and scream for a bit, but that would be too stereotyped if he just fought off the wolf that way. Besides, they need to fill in more time. There's still twenty minutes left in the movie. They'll fight for awhile, then at the last minute the wolf will overcome him. I'll bet just as the wolf is going for his throat, she's going to whack the wolf with a stick and save the day. See the stick? It's just sitting there, too convenient.

I can almost see the sign on it that says 'grab me.' And you'll notice her ankle won't be so sprained anymore."

They continued to watch as the scene continued to unfold. Janice gasped and brought both hands to her mouth as the movie heroine, a terrible actress whose name Trevor couldn't remember and didn't care to remember, eventually did exactly as he predicted.

"You're right! How did you know? Did you read a review or something with some animal activist group complaining about this cruel mistreatment?" Janice turned and glared at him, but he could tell she was only pretending to be angry.

Trevor grinned and pointed as discreetly as he could to the corner of the screen so as not to disturb others around them. "Naw. The wolf is as fake as the boulder that nearly hit them. Look at the tail."

They put their heads together, ear to ear, and Trevor described the many flaws of the fake animal, as well as the mathematically perfect tear that suddenly appeared in the hero's shirt, exposing his manly hairy chest for the female viewing audience.

Janice giggled again.

"Will you two knock it off?" Laura hissed. "I'm trying to watch this!"

Trevor slipped his arm over the back of the chair behind Janice, just so he could lean over more easily to whisper in her ear again. "I think we'd better behave, or we're going to be in trouble."

Janice raised her index finger, pressed it to her lips, and nodded.

Since she didn't flinch away from him, Trevor neglected to remove his arm. When she didn't complain after a minute, he moved just a little and rested his palm on her shoulder. To his surprise and delight, she still didn't protest, so he decided to keep it there and just be quiet and watch the rest of the movie.

As the scene progressed, once the hero and heroine were assured the big bad wolf was dead, they hugged and kissed to end the traumatic life-threatening episode. Both Trevor and Janice had to muffle their laughter as the evil forest ranger villain, rifle in hand, appeared conveniently and predictably too late, only to find out he didn't get the girl in the end.

Beside Janice, Laura sniffled at what was probably supposed to be a very touching scene. Beside Laura, Frank appeared to be on the verge of falling asleep.

And then the credits started to roll.

Despite the pathetic special effects, the questionable acting, and the nonexistent plot, Trevor couldn't remember the last time he'd enjoyed a movie so much.

Janice leaned toward him, so he leaned toward her to meet in the middle.

"That was really funny. You know, if we rent that someday to watch it again, we'll probably wonder why we thought it was good the first time around."

"Probably." He smiled, thinking about her use of the word "we" and wondering if she realized what she'd just said.

"The arm around me was a nice touch. However, the movie's over. Now move it off before I smack it off."

Trevor hesitated. Part of him wanted to keep his hand there, just to see if she really would smack it off. But then again, she had some kind of higher belt in martial arts. Instead of hitting like a pansy, she could probably deliver a punch that broke bones as well as boards. Then again, if she said she wouldn't flatten him in the privacy of her living room, she likely wouldn't flatten him in a public movie theater.

Thinking of the incident in the living room, he remembered how he'd unwittingly reminded her of something that had frightened or hurt her very badly in the past.

In the blink of an eye, Trevor removed his hand.

Frank became more alert once people started exiting the theater, then fully awake by the time they walked outside and into the fresh evening air. Fully invigorated and refreshed after his nap, Frank suggested that instead of taking the women home, they detour to the local donut shop. They all piled into Frank's car, Frank and Laura in the front, and Trevor in the backseat with Janice.

Trevor scanned the distance on the seat between them, and for a second he experienced a fleeting sense of jealousy. When the four of them had gone together in Janice's small economy import car, Frank and Laura were forced to sit close together in the backseat. In the back of Frank's large car, Janice positioned herself almost squashed against the door, and there seemed to be miles between them. He started daydreaming about taking Janice's car the next time they went somewhere, only asking Laura to drive so he and Janice could get the backseat.

As Trevor realized where his thoughts were leading, Frank pulled into a parking spot. They all piled out and went into the donut shop. Back on track, Trevor tried to point the conversation to Friday night's couples' counseling sessions and the upcoming wedding. Instead they talked about everything else, most notably nothing that could in any way be important.

Not that he didn't have a nice time, but he wasn't there to have a nice time. Even though the wedding was still a little over three months away, he was starting to see that Janice might have been right to be so worried so soon. Nothing they had done was making any headway between Frank and Laura. Neither one of them had changed, nor did they appear likely to in the near—or distant—future. The worst part was that they both acted so out of character with each other. As the pastor had said, thinking you were going to change your partner after the wedding was a dangerous notion because it wasn't likely to happen.

Worse for Frank and Laura, neither of them knew there was anything to change. Both of them were acting totally out of character, yet they were the only ones who couldn't see it. When the day came that they stopped being so accommodating to each other and more like themselves, they were both in for the shock of a lifetime. More than ever, Trevor became determined to be sure that happened before the wedding.

The next time the four of them went together to a show, he would pick something he knew Frank liked, then watch how Laura dealt with it. He would bet that with all the action, Laura wouldn't fall asleep like Frank had. He also doubted she would enjoy such a movie, although he thought Janice might.

Trevor watched Janice and Frank play-arguing about the chocolate sprinkles on the donuts while Laura stirred her coffee and stared out the window at an animated billboard. While the movie was understatedly bad, Trevor couldn't imagine himself falling asleep with Janice beside him like Frank had with Laura. Janice may not have been the most charming date, but she was fun to be with, and there was never a dull moment.

Laura stood, and Frank and Janice fell silent. "I hate to be a party pooper, but we all have to get up for church in the morning."

Trevor nodded as he also checked his watch. "That's right, and we're going to our church this time." He turned, making direct eye contact with Janice as he spoke. "And remember, my church is a little more conservative than yours." He didn't elaborate further. The slacks she wore to the office would have been fine, but what he really wanted was for Janice to wear that dress again.

Janice didn't comment. Trevor knew he'd fall asleep dreaming of Janice in that blue dress.

The trip back to Janice and Laura's house seemed too short. Before he knew it, Frank and Laura were sharing a short good-bye kiss in the front seat, and Janice was standing outside the car with the door wide open.

Before closing the door, she rested her hands on the roof of the car and leaned down, speaking to him from across the length of the backseat. "Conservative, huh? I hope I don't have to wear a tie."

His mouth tightened. "Not funny," he grumbled. "You'll have to wear something nice, though."

Suddenly, her frown turned into a smile that was a little too bright. "Don't worry. I'll try to find some good jeans that don't have a hole in the knee," she said and hopped backward a step.

He leaned over and opened his mouth to tell her not to wear jeans at all, but the car door closed in his face. Janice ran into the house, with Laura walking slowly behind.

Suddenly, the donut he'd previously thought so delicious went to war with his stomach.

Trevor climbed into the front seat with Frank, and they drove home.

He knew it was going to be a long night.

❧

Trevor stood beside Frank on Janice and Laura's doorstep and raised his fist to knock. At the exact same moment as he started the downward motion, the door opened. He stepped back quickly, barely missing whacking Laura on the head as she ran past him.

"Sorry," she mumbled, only slowing slightly. "I just got a call to do an emergency fill-in at Sunday school."

Frank turned in an instant. "I'll go with you. Do you need some help in the class?"

"That would be great. Let's go. I have to set up, and people will already be arriving."

Trevor turned and watched Frank and Laura jog down the sidewalk. "But we were supposed to go to my church today. I'm helping with the offering, so I can't go to your church today."

Laura hopped into the passenger's seat of Frank's car, calling out to him as she closed the door. "Sorry. You and Janice can still go, though. See you sometime during the week. Bye."

Both doors closed with a muffled thud, and Frank drove off.

"Trevor? Is that you?" Janice called from within the house.

He stepped inside and shut the door behind him. "Yeah. I guess it's just you and me. Apparently, I'm at your mercy for transportation. Frank just left with Laura."

He could hear Janice's footsteps in the hall. For an instant, a vision of Janice wearing jeans and her ratty sneakers flashed through his mind. He steeled his nerves and waited.

Trevor's breath caught as Janice stepped into his sight. Instead of the jeans he'd half expected, she wore a casual skirt and blouse. After he got over the shock, he noticed it was a denim skirt. A jean skirt.

He couldn't help but grin. "You are a brat. I should have expected something like that out of you."

She grinned back. "I hate wearing skirts, but it was worth it just to see the look on your face. I'm ready. Let's go."

While he waited for her to lock up, Trevor couldn't help but think back to what he'd said the night before. He should have realized Janice would have taken his request that she wear something nice as a challenge. Part of him told himself never to make that mistake again, and part of him thought it was hilarious.

He also wondered what he could do to make the most of it.

During the drive to his church, he did his best to answer her questions. Many of them served as a reminder that Janice had only been a Christian a few years, whereas he'd been in a Christian family all his life, as had Frank. They had both made their decisions to follow Jesus in their teens.

He heard Janice inhale deeply the second he turned into the church's parking lot.

"This is where you go?"

He'd attended this same church with his family all his life. He gazed up at the grand old stone building and tried to think of how a newcomer would see it. Without a doubt, the building was impressive. The stained glass windows alone were breathtaking. As a child, when he was bored with the service, he often let his attention wander to the craftsmanship of the colorful antique windows. From an adult's perspective, now that he knew the time and workmanship involved, especially in the day they were made, they impressed him even more.

"Yeah. Pretty nice, isn't it? Wait 'til you see the inside. It's a heritage building, and it's very well cared for. Up until about a year ago, an elderly lady even played the big old pipe organ on

Sundays. But she retired, and now we have a piano and a guitar. No drums or anything like at your church, though. It's just a big, black, grand piano and an amplified acoustic guitar. I also want you to take notice that every male over the age of thirteen is wearing a tie."

When they made their way inside, Trevor had to bite his lip and not laugh. Janice didn't say a word. She just looked around the building, in complete and total awe of her surroundings.

He didn't know why he did it. Maybe because she was so pretty wearing nice clothes for a change. Maybe out of respect for his surroundings. Admittedly, most of the members of his congregation were older, and with their age, old-fashioned. It just felt right. Trevor picked up Janice's hand and tucked it into the crook of his elbow, resting his hand on top of hers as he gave her a tour of the building.

From a distance, as they walked around, Janice saw her old boss and his wife. They waved at each other pleasantly, and Trevor led Janice into the sanctuary, where they took their seats in the polished wooden pews.

Pastor Gregory soon welcomed everyone present, highlighting a few items from the bulletin, and the worship leader stepped forward. Janice participated eagerly in the worship time, during which the congregation sang mostly hymns and a couple of contemporary choruses. Trevor felt bad about leaving her while he helped accept the morning's offering. In their original plan, she wouldn't have been left alone because Frank and Laura were supposed to be there too. However, her graciousness impressed him. He didn't think he'd ever forget her cute little smile and wink when he passed the basket by her, and she tucked something inside.

She remained quiet beside him for the rest of the service, paying rapt attention as the pastor spoke. At the close of the service, he led Janice into the lobby.

Perhaps because he'd had her holding onto him before the service, she automatically did the same as they walked around afterward. The contact of her warm hand on his arm made him in no rush to leave.

As they continued to walk around, they alternated between making small talk with people he knew to privately discussing more of the points of interest in the heritage building and features of the church as a body of believers. He'd always enjoyed the majesty of the old place and felt the surroundings greatly added to the mood of worship to his Lord and Savior.

The more they continued to walk around, the more Trevor noticed people's heads turning.

He tipped his head to talk softly to Janice as she checked out a table of featured books from the church's library. "You know, I think people are looking at us funny."

"They are? Why? I'm properly dressed."

Trevor shook his head. "I don't know. Maybe it's because I've never brought a woman to church before. That's kind of an indication of a serious relationship, which no one knew I was having. Of course, I didn't know I was having a serious relationship either."

Janice stopped flipping pages and turned to smile up at him as she spoke. He hadn't noticed before that moment that the room had been getting a little warm.

"That's okay," she said. "I suppose this is the kind of thing we should expect if we're going to pull this off with Frank and Laura. Just be sure to act suitably heartbroken when we break up, and everything will be fine."

He'd already thought about officially splitting up with Janice after Frank and Laura finally saw the light. Suddenly, a queasy feeling settled in the pit of his stomach. He raised his wrist to check his watch to see if it was close to lunchtime.

While he stared blankly at his watch, he heard someone calling his name.

Suddenly, his stomach felt even worse. "Oh, no," he mumbled. "This is something I hadn't thought about."

"Huh?" Janice mumbled as she continued to page through the book in her hand.

"It would have been different if we were here with Frank

and Laura, but we're alone."

"So?" She closed the book and returned it to its place on the table.

"It's totally obvious we're together."

"I thought that was the point." She picked up another book and started reading the back cover.

"It's my parents. They see that we're together, and they're coming to talk to us. I have a bad feeling they're going to invite us over for lunch. When they do that on Sunday, I always go."

She smiled so sweetly, his poor stomach didn't know how to feel. "What's wrong with that? They're your parents."

"You don't understand. By now, they will have talked to my sister, who can never keep her mouth shut. I can tell by the way my mom's walking toward us that she's got something on her mind. That means Melissa told them I'm going to a pre-marital course. Since I haven't told my parents I was even seeing someone on a regular basis, they're going to want to know what's going on. I'm twenty-five years old, and Mom's been hinting for awhile that it's about time I got married."

Janice stiffened from head to toe. "Uh-oh. . . ," she muttered.

Trevor dropped his voice to a whisper. "Here they come. Remember. We're supposed to be in love."

ten

Janice forced herself to breathe.

Love.

She didn't know what it was like to be in love. Her heart didn't do silly flip-flops when she was around Trevor. She didn't count the minutes and seconds until the next time she would see him again. She didn't dream about him; at least she didn't dream about him very much.

She tried to give herself a crash course on being in love. She tried to think of everything listed in 1 Corinthians 13, but she'd never actually memorized it.

"Love is patient; love is kind. Love doesn't boast. It is not self-seeking."

Mentally, Janice shook her head. She couldn't remember any more, and what she did remember was undoubtedly in the wrong order with many traits missing. The order didn't matter anyway. She didn't know how those things actually related to the way someone felt in their heart about a person they were supposed to be in love with. She thought she'd been in love once before; but after she and her boyfriend split up, she realized it wasn't love at all but an infatuation, over as quickly as it began.

As Trevor's parents approached, she could see they were both tall and both fairly good-looking for their age. She estimated them to be in their early sixties, both by their appearance and because Trevor was the youngest of four children. She could also see that Trevor got his nose from his father's side of the family.

"Hi, Mom. Dad. I'd like you to meet Janice. Janice, these are my parents, Ed and Kathy."

Janice tried to smile politely, and they smiled back.

Suddenly, she was extremely grateful for the book in her hand. She didn't know if she was supposed to shake their hands or if there was something else she should have done. Also, since she was supposed to be having a serious relationship with their son, she didn't know if she was supposed to call them by their first names, their last names, or. . .Mom and Dad.

"Pleased to meet you, Mr. and Mrs. Halliday," she mumbled through her forced smile.

Mrs. Halliday glanced back and forth between them, and Janice couldn't help but wonder what she was thinking.

"It's a pleasure to meet you, Janice. Melissa told us all about you and Trevor. To tell the truth, we didn't even know that Trevor was seeing anyone, so it's good to meet up with you today."

Trevor didn't speak, but his face said, "I told you so."

Janice found herself waiting for the lunch invitation, undecided about what she should do. She thought it might be fun to accept, just to watch Trevor's response—after all, he was the one who had gotten them into this situation.

Then again, she didn't want to put Trevor in an awkward position. Even though they hadn't known each other well at first, only being casual acquaintances at the beginning of their supposed relationship, things had changed. She now appreciated and valued his friendship.

All she did was smile. Whatever happened, she would let Trevor handle it and go along with his decision, although she suspected that he was looking to her to give him an easy out.

Mrs. Halliday glanced at Trevor, then back to Janice. "Any other day, we would have loved to have you both over for lunch. However, we've already accepted an invitation from Walter and Ellen Quinlan."

Janice nearly choked. She wasn't going to tell them that Walter was her boss before he retired and gave the company reins to his nephew, Ken.

Trying to be discreet, she glanced to the side. She couldn't see him now, but Walter had already seen her with Trevor. Knowing Walter, she had no doubt that if Walter thought about it, an invitation to them would be forthcoming, especially since she already knew him, and Trevor's parents had already accepted their invitation. If Walter found out how allegedly serious her relationship with Trevor was supposed to be, Walter would tell Ken because Ken was now her boss.

Not that Ken spread gossip, but Ken would certainly tell his wife Molly. Janice had worked closely with Molly—Molly had been the one to lead her to Jesus. Janice had also been awarded Molly's job when Molly and Ken got married. Janice had no doubt that news of her personal life would be welcome news to Molly.

While Molly no longer worked for Quinlan Enterprises, she often showed up at the office and remained friendly with all the staff. Once Molly got wind that she and Trevor were an item, Janice easily pictured Molly orchestrating a surprise bridal shower at the office.

Besides misleading Trevor's parents, this was another complication neither of them needed.

Janice cleared her throat. "You know, Trevor, we really should be going. We're going to be late. I didn't notice the time."

Trevor's eyebrows arched. "Late?"

Janice nudged him in the ankle with her toe. "Yes. We're going to be late."

"Oh. Yes. You're right. Excuse us, please, Mom and Dad. We've got to go. Maybe we can get together another time."

Both Mr. and Mrs. Halliday smiled brightly.

Mr. Halliday patted Trevor on the shoulder. "Catch you another time, Trev."

Guilt a foot thick piled on Janice's head. She remained silent. She also made a mental note that Trevor's father didn't seem to talk much, and she wondered briefly if once he got started, he too would be hard to turn off.

Trevor's mother smiled sweetly and rested her hand on his

father's arm. "We'll have to make plans to get together for coffee one evening, or maybe after church next weekend?"

"Sure, Mom. Now if you'll excuse us."

Janice smiled, returned the book to the table, then hustled out of the building with Trevor, straight to her car without speaking to anyone else.

Trevor didn't speak until they were standing beside her car. "What is it we're late for?" he asked.

"I don't know. Lunch, I guess." Janice heaved a huge sigh of relief.

Trevor checked his watch. "I wonder if we should try to find Frank and Laura."

"I don't know." Janice grabbed the door handle but didn't open the door. "Part of me says we have to try harder to get them to see each other in a more realistic light, but part of me says to leave them alone for awhile. Maybe they need some time without us, so they can start some of this discovery stuff mentioned in that booklet we got on Friday night. I honestly don't know what to do anymore."

She slid inside, reached over to unlock the passenger door for Trevor, and they drove off. Glancing out the corner of her eye, she realized Trevor had turned toward her and was watching her intently as she drove.

"What?" she asked, glancing quickly at him, then returning her attention to the traffic around them.

"I know we keep saying we have to talk, but you know what? We never do. I mean really talk. There is something I feel we should discuss, and I don't want to do it in a moving car or with Frank and Laura or anyone else we know looming. I also don't want to need to watch the time."

"What are you saying?"

"Instead of going to where we know Frank and Laura will probably be, let's do the opposite. Let's go someplace we know they won't be. Someplace private, where we can talk uninterrupted and without an audience. For as long as it takes."

Her grip on the steering wheel tightened. "You mean, go to

my place? Since we know Laura won't be home?"

"No. I'm not positive they won't go straight to your place after lunch. Same thing with my place. Maybe they'll go there; maybe they won't. Trouble is, I don't know where to go. I really don't want to go to a public restaurant either. Or anywhere that there's a crowd."

"You're not leaving a lot of options here. If you want private, it's not going to happen. If you've got something to say, say it now, in the car. But I don't want to get into a heavy discussion that will compromise my concentration on my driving. And I'm starving. Stress always makes me hungry."

Trevor snapped his fingers. "The car! That's it!"

"Pardon me?"

"Let's go to a drive-in restaurant. We can still get our lunches served to us but not be in a room full of people. We won't have to worry about being interrupted by someone we know because we'll be sitting in the car. No one will bug us, and we can take as long as we want. It's perfect."

Janice grinned. "Great idea. I haven't been to a drive-in restaurant since I was a kid. I always go to the drive-thru window and take it home."

Immediately, she turned and headed for the drive-in restaurant she'd gone to as a child. She picked a spot on the end, away from the majority of the other cars, and killed the engine. They didn't waste any time, quickly decided what they wanted, and ordered.

The second the carhop left, Janice turned in the seat toward Trevor, resting one arm over the top of the steering wheel. "Okay. Here we are, all alone. Talk."

Trevor cleared his throat and paused, giving her a bad feeling that she wasn't going to like what he was about to say.

"I've been thinking. What if we're wrong? What if Frank and Laura really are more suited to each other than we think?"

At his words, Janice didn't know which she felt more: hungry or sick. She removed her arm from over the steering wheel and clasped the steering wheel with both hands.

Her voice came out in a strange squeak. "This is scary. I've been thinking the same thing myself. For everything we point out to them, they don't seem to think any of it matters. What if those things aren't as important to a relationship as I always thought? If God has put them together, who are we to separate them?"

Trevor's face tightened. "I know. But there's another side of it too. What if we're right, and they're only fooling themselves for reasons we can't figure out? What kind of friends would we be if we stood back and just let them set their lives up for heartbreak and misery?"

Janice nodded. "I know that in any relationship, realistically, two people will never share every common interest. If they did, then life would eventually become too boring for words. But those two have taken the 'opposites attract' thing to the extreme."

He nodded. "There has to be a middle ground, but those two aren't in it—at least not that I can see. But I'm not as sure that marriage isn't what God wants for them as I was a couple of weeks ago."

"Then I suppose the best thing to do is what we've already been doing. To point out where couples should agree, where it's good to have a different approach, focus on common interests and personality traits, and let them discover the truth for themselves. We'll have to support them whatever happens, whether they get married, or they split up. We're doing everything we can."

"Not really. There is one thing we've been missing so far."

Janice frowned. "What? I've thought so carefully about this. I've participated with you in what we agree is the best course of action. We've got them involved with the pastor and a good, in-depth session that's exactly what they need to get to know each other deep down. I'm continuing to pray about Laura and Frank every day. I don't know what else to do."

He leaned back in the confines of her small car, shuffled his feet, then crossed his arms over his chest. Oddly, the action made him appear even larger. "We've both prayed about Frank and Laura separately, but we haven't prayed together. I think it's long overdue."

She gulped. Of course he was right. They did need to pray together. They should have prayed together when they first began their efforts.

A tap on the window brought their attention to the carhop holding their tray of food outside, another stark reminder of being constantly interrupted. However, this time, when the carhop left they were finally, exclusively alone in their own, enclosed world.

Trevor wasted no time and immediately prayed over their meal. While they ate the conversation changed. They didn't talk at all about Frank and Laura, which Janice found a welcome diversion and a much-needed break.

Lately, the strange mismatch had been occupying her thoughts day and night. Whenever she had been able to free her mind from thoughts of Frank and Laura, her thoughts strayed to Trevor. She didn't know why, but she attributed the phenomenon to his proximity and involvement with the situation.

When they were finished eating, Janice moved all the wrappers and empty mugs to the tray hanging on her window, but she didn't turn on the headlights to signal the carhop to come.

They were finally ready to do what should have been done a long time ago.

"I want to pray intelligently," she said as she rolled the window up most of the way, leaving it only open enough to give them some fresh air. "I also want to be sure that we're both praying for the same thing before we start. After all, it's been some time since this whole thing blew up in our faces. Since then, I'd think a few things have changed, even if our bottom-line goal hasn't. I have to admit it feels very strange, praying with someone else about being a part in trying to break off the engagement of my best friend."

He nodded. "I know. I've been feeling the same way. Maybe that's why we've put off praying together for so long."

All Janice could do was nod back.

Trevor smiled for only a brief second, then became serious. He reached over the stick shift and grasped her hands in his. "First and foremost, we want to be sure we are in God's will for this. Whether they break up, or whether they actually do get married, I want to be obedient to do whatever God wants to happen here in this situation."

"Yes, that's most important. We do have to accept the possibility that they'll stay together, even though we think it won't work. God's plan is bigger than our plan, and He sees things we don't."

Trevor nodded again. "Sometimes I forget that. I need the occasional reminder, I think."

Janice thought she needed reminders too. However, with both of them more aware of each other's weaknesses, she became more confident that they could keep each other on track by working together more and being less independent. "I still think we're doing the right thing. We're not openly or aggressively trying to make them split up. We're only helping them get to know each other better, which is a good thing, especially if they do decide to go through with the wedding. That couples' course was a great idea. I think it may even have been God's timing. I'm almost positive that will be what they need to show them they're not right for each other. All we need to do is keep after them and make sure they do the assignments and really talk about stuff, like Pastor Harry says to do. That's the only way they'll get to know each other properly. But you know that means we have to do the same thing, right along with them."

For a minute, he remained silent. "I know," he said, then became silent again.

Janice waited for him to say more, but he didn't, nor did he appear to be waiting for her to say anything. They simply sat there, staring at each other within the closed car, the only movement being the slow back and forth motion of his thumbs on her wrists as his large hands completely enveloped hers.

They were kind of holding hands, but kind of not, since he was the one doing all the holding. Yet, she could have pulled away at any time because he really didn't have any grip on her. His big hands were more wrapped around hers than holding them. She should have felt strange, touching like that, sitting with no words between them, but in a strange way Janice enjoyed it. They had all the time in the world. Not needing to speak and not feeling awkward about it felt strangely right. Comfortable. His lazy half grin told her that he felt the same way.

The more time they spent together, the more she'd come to appreciate him. Spending so much time together and digging deep into both her psyche and his, as the couples' course required, wasn't so scary anymore. Despite his size, he was kind and gentle. Yet, at the same time, when he really wanted something, she had sampled his dogged determination first-hand. While he didn't have an upper-management career, he accepted much responsibility with his various duties and seemed to be proficient at a job he enjoyed. Most of all, she thoroughly enjoyed his offbeat sense of humor and often wondered why Laura didn't seem to have much patience with him, which had been obvious at the movie theater.

As the minutes passed, his lazy-cat expression turned into more of a grin, and those adorable little crinkles she was becoming so fond of appeared at the corners of his sparkling blue eyes. Watching the little crinkles appear made her aware that she had been staring into his eyes for quite some time and hadn't realized it. She didn't know when or why she had become so fascinated with Trevor's eyes. She'd always thought that the typical female attraction to men with blue eyes was highly overrated.

His quirky little grin became infectious. Before she knew it, Janice felt herself starting to grin too, even though she didn't know why.

Finally, Janice couldn't stand it anymore. She had to break the silence. "What are you thinking about?"

The smile dropped. He cleared his throat, dropped her hands, and sat straight in the seat. "Nothing. Is there anything else we need to talk about before we pray?"

The brusque way he switched moods to the business at hand left her with her mouth gaping open. Abruptly, she snapped it shut and turned to stare out the windshield as she tried to figure out if she'd said or done something to make him angry. Not that he appeared angry; she'd never seen him angry. The problem was that she didn't know what he felt, and it bothered her that she might have been the cause of it.

She turned back to face him. "I can't think of anything else."

"Okay," he mumbled.

Silence hung between them.

Janice focused all her attention on his hands, which were now folded in his lap. She wanted the same thing they had only a few minutes ago. Not only did she want to join their hands while they prayed, something deep inside her needed to do so. She also wanted the warmth between them back.

If he wasn't going to take the initiative, then she was left with no alternative.

Janice leaned forward, lifted up his hands, tried her best to cover his hands with hers, and gave them a gentle squeeze.

She smiled. "You ready?"

Trevor smiled back and moved his hands so their fingers were intertwined. "Yeah."

Something funny happened in her stomach, which Janice couldn't figure out because she'd just eaten a wonderful meal and her tummy was well-satisfied.

She cleared her throat. "You want to start?"

"Sure."

They both bowed their heads, taking a minute to clear their minds and hearts, and Trevor began to pray for their situation. He prayed for God's continued guidance, for Frank and Laura to respond to God's leading, and for themselves—to be within God's will, and to be able to accept the outcome of their efforts, whatever it might be.

All Janice could do was agree and say "Amen."

For the first time since she'd heard the news of Frank and Laura's engagement, Janice felt at peace.

Their fingers separated, and they both sat straight in their seats.

Janice turned on the headlights. Within minutes, a carhop removed the tray from the window, and they were ready to go.

"That's it, then," she said as she started the engine. "Now we continue to do what we've been doing, but this time it's in Someone else's hands, where it should have been all along."

Trevor nodded. "Yup. So, tomorrow's Monday. Any idea what we're all supposed to be doing?"

Janice bit back a grin. "I heard rumors of bowling."

"Bowling! Please, don't do that to me!"

Janice pulled into traffic. "But think of how much fun we had last time."

Trevor groaned. She simply listened in silence as he complained the entire trip back to his house.

eleven

"Good afternoon, Quinlan Enterprises."

Trevor turned to try to block the sound of a truck going by. "Hi, Janice."

"Trevor? Are you on a roof somewhere again?"

He grinned openly, even though he was technically alone. "Can you tell?"

"Yes. Why are you calling? Do you have good news? Laura didn't say anything to me this morning. Everything was all normal."

His grin dropped. "Actually, I was calling to see what you're doing tonight."

A silence hung over the phone for a few seconds.

"I didn't think we were doing anything this evening. Laura has a Sunday school teacher's meeting. Remember?"

Trevor blocked the mouthpiece with his hand as another truck approached on the street below. "I didn't forget. I wasn't thinking of going out with Frank and Laura. I was just asking you."

This time, the silence on the phone seemed to last forever.

"Me?" she finally squeaked out.

"Yes, you."

More silence loomed.

He'd hoped for a more enthusiastic response, but he supposed he had this coming. It had been two months since they began their mission to talk some sense into Frank and Laura. In all that time he'd only been out alone with Janice once, the day he took her to his church, and their time together that day had been far from planned. All they'd done was sit in her car to eat and pray, which had been badly needed at the time.

That had been a month ago. Since then, the only other time

124

they hadn't been with Frank and Laura they had gone to visit his parents, and that didn't count. He'd been so nervous he hadn't been able to think straight.

He'd introduced Janice as his girlfriend, but he could tell that his parents, especially his mother, had been sitting on the edges of their seats, waiting for him to hint at promises of future wedding bells. Of course, it didn't happen.

Janice had handled the uncomfortable evening better than he had. Instead of letting them dwell on the disappointment that their son wasn't announcing an engagement after all, she cleverly turned the conversation to the progression of plans for Frank and Laura's wedding, which sufficiently distracted his mother. Before he knew it, they were in the car, waving their good-byes.

All the way home she'd teased him mercilessly about his predicament with his parents and even laughed. He'd thought the evening had been anything but funny. In retrospect, he appreciated it more, now that some time had passed.

Fortunately, they wouldn't have to deal with her parents, since they lived in a different city about five hundred miles away. By the time they arrived for Frank and Laura's wedding, if it happened, everything would be over, and life would be back to normal.

And now, he didn't want life to get back to normal. The better he got to know Janice the more he enjoyed being with her, even with Frank and Laura present every time they did something together. However, he could do something about that, if he really wanted to.

Since she still hadn't said anything, Trevor decided to forge ahead anyway.

He cleared his throat. "I thought it would be kind of fun to go out, just the two of us, for a change."

Another silence hung on the line.

If he had to be honest with himself, he had been thinking of what it would be like to go out and do things without Frank and Laura present for a long time. However, they'd been so busy going out as a foursome the opportunity had never come up.

Last night he had sat home alone waiting to call her after she got back from her exercise class. After realizing what he was doing and why, he came to the conclusion that sometimes opportunities had to be made.

"I guess. . . ," she mumbled.

"Great. I'll pick you up at six, and we'll go for dinner. And wear jeans. Okay?"

"Uh. . . Okay. . . . Oops. I have another call coming in. I-have-to-go-bye."

A click sounded, and the dial tone buzzed in his ear.

As he pushed the End button on his cell phone, Trevor caught himself smiling at her rushed end to the conversation.

For the rest of the afternoon, he found himself anticipating the evening. He already knew where they were going to go and what they were going to do. He only hoped he was ready.

At six o'clock sharp, he knocked on Janice's door with one hand behind his back.

She answered, wearing a plain pink blouse and a nice pair of jeans—without a hole in the knee. He'd seen the blouse before as something she wore to work. The simplicity of it suited her.

"Hi." Trevor smiled and brought his hand forward.

Her eyebrows raised, and she tipped her head up to make eye contact. "What's that?"

Trevor sighed. "They're called flowers, Janice."

"What are they for?"

"When a man gives flowers to a lady prior to going out together, it's usually taken as a sign of affection."

"Oh." She stared at them like they were made of toxic residue. Then her cheeks darkened. "Thank you. I guess I should put them in water or something. Come in for a minute."

He stepped inside and waited beside the door until she returned.

"Where are we going?"

"I thought we'd go to that café in Stanley Park for a nice little dinner, then walk around the park for awhile. The weather is warm and the days are getting longer, so I thought that would be a good end to a nice spring day."

Her little smile warmed his heart. "That sounds nice."

They made pleasant small talk on the long drive to the park. The parking lot had many wide-open spaces, and the restaurant itself was busy but not crowded, exactly as he expected for a spring weeknight.

He'd never been inside, but he'd heard the restaurant was quaint, the food good, and overall, it was a great place to take a woman for a quiet and informal evening.

She tugged on his sleeve as soon as they walked in the door. "Wow. Look at this place. Are you sure about this?"

He grinned down at her. "I hope you like seafood."

"I do, but this place is so, well, you know. If we're just going to walk around, why don't we go to the concession stand by the beach and get a couple of hot dogs?"

"Why don't we get a nice cozy table for two on the patio and walk around later?"

She shuffled to stand closer to him as she continued to study the decor. Her voice dropped to a near whisper. "I don't know, Trevor. This place seems so, I don't know, kind of romantic."

"What's wrong with that?"

"But it's just us."

"I know. That's why I picked it. I thought it would be a nice change. And I don't want to hear any arguments like you usually do about paying. This is my treat because it was my idea. And since I'm driving, one word from you about money and you can walk home."

"If you want to waste your money, that's fine with me. Just don't complain when I pick the most expensive thing on the menu."

He grinned and said nothing, knowing she was kidding. He actually wouldn't have minded if she did order something expensive. He wanted tonight to be special—for a number of reasons.

After they were seated at a table and had placed their order, Trevor pulled the booklet from the previous session of the couples' counseling course out of his back pocket. "I also thought this would be a good place to do our homework."

"Good idea." Janice pulled her rather scrunched-up booklet out of her purse, then began to dig to the bottom for the two pens she always carried. "Class is tomorrow, and I haven't even looked at the assignment yet," she muttered as she dug through her purse. "The days are sure going fast, aren't they?"

"Yes." He watched as she began pulling stuff out of her purse in her quest for the pens. First she pulled out a notepad, then a collapsible umbrella, a fork, a map, a squashed-up church bulletin from a month ago, a screwdriver, her day planner, an empty mesh shopping bag, and a computer disk. She located one of the pens, then continued to pull out smaller items, including a couple of Scrabble tiles and other items. He couldn't for the life of him figure out why the last few items were in her purse.

She did the same thing every time she hunted for the pens, only not to this extreme. He didn't know why she didn't clip the pens inside the day planner, which was always one of the first things out of her purse. Every time she went through the same process to find something, he wondered, even anticipated, what else got loaded in there over the past few days. Judging from the volume of clutter on the table, the thing was a bottomless pit.

He knew he'd seen something most men never saw—the contents of a woman's purse. One of life's timeless mysteries, solved.

Trevor plunked his elbows on the little remaining visible tabletop and cupped his chin in his palms. "Why don't you just carry a suitcase? Then you could really take along everything you need from day to day, including a change of clothes. Unless you have that in there too, but you haven't got that far down yet."

She grumbled something he wasn't sure he wanted to hear.

She found the second pen and shoved everything back into her purse only seconds before the waiter arrived with their meals. After Trevor led with a short prayer of thanks, they both paged to the assignment and rested the open booklets on the table and began to eat. He didn't want to remind her that it was rude to read at the table when with someone. He'd been the one to prepare ahead and had already reviewed both the lesson and the assignment.

"I remember now," Janice mumbled through her mouthful as she flipped the pages, scanning the material from the previous week. "The last lesson was on trust, and we were supposed to practice trusting each other."

Trevor fiddled with his fork, then laid it down so he wouldn't appear too nervous. "I know we don't have the same kind of relationship or the future plans as everyone else in that class, but over the last couple of months I think I can safely say we've at least become friends. With any friendship there is a good degree of trust. So it's kind of the same but kind of different. When I read what we're supposed to do this week, I found I do trust you like that."

She smiled and laid her own fork down. "That's so sweet of you to say that. I trust you too."

He forced himself to smile. "Before you say that, you should really read what the book says to do."

Janice scrunched her eyebrows, reached up to adjust her glasses, then flipped a few pages forward. "Hmm. . .I haven't read the whole thing, but this first part is so basic it's childish. They ask if I trust you with my safety. It says that I'm supposed to close my eyes and fall backward and trust you to catch me. What a silly thing to do."

"Maybe, but it says to do it. I trust you to catch me when I fall backward."

Janice made a very unladylike snort and closed the booklet.

"Then we can do our homework after supper. That's not something we can do in a restaurant. Is that why you wanted to come to the wide-open park? So I would land on the soft ground if you missed me? I know I'm going to catch you."

Her little grin eased some of the growing tremor of anticipation in his stomach. He sipped his water and nibbled on his salmon to try to ease the sensation a little more. It was the second part of the assignment that was the reason he'd brought her to the park.

"Very funny. I wanted to be completely alone in a relaxed atmosphere, and there's nothing more relaxing than being outside in the middle of the beauty of God's creation. You know, the breeze and the fresh ocean air in our faces, the sounds of the seagulls squawking overhead, and the waves lapping up the shore. The promise of the new growth of spring in the trees around us. . ."

Her eyes widened, as if she couldn't believe what he was saying. "I guess," she muttered, then lowered her head and resumed eating.

Trevor grinned. Between the cozy dinner for two and the romantic setting of the ocean park, most women would have been eating out his hand. But not Janice. He'd never seen a woman so unromantic as Janice. She hadn't gushed over the flowers, she never seemed anxious to see him, and she never tried to impress him. He remembered back to the evening she'd closed the door in his face when he'd playfully tried to kiss her good night. Janice was also the most pragmatic person he'd ever met. He'd never known a woman could be so focused and determined once she set her mind to something, whether it was to straighten out Frank and Laura or if it was to follow the manual and change the spark plugs in her own car.

Since theirs was not a typical dating relationship, he couldn't expect her to do the usual things, but Janice was not a woman to be stereotyped. He couldn't even say she did the opposite of everything he expected because now, knowing her as he did, he did expect most of her reactions and opinions. He also accepted that hers were different than any other woman he'd dated.

At the thought of dating Janice, he nearly choked on his mouthful and had to quickly take a sip of water. He wasn't dating Janice. The relationship had been fabricated from the beginning. However, one thing could not be fabricated, and that was the growth of their very real friendship.

"This was delicious. Thank you, Trevor."

"You're welcome. Would you like dessert?"

"No. I think we should just go outside, catch each other, and then go for a walk before it gets dark out. I don't come here very often, and this is a real treat."

Trevor led Janice to a quiet, grassy spot beneath a large patch of cedar trees. "The book says that this is supposed to demonstrate trust in our physical needs, to show we trust the other to help when we need it."

She made that snorting sound again and dropped her purse to the ground. "If you say so. Okay, here I come. You ready?"

Because she was so short Trevor lowered himself to one knee. When he held his hands out in front of him, she smiled, closed her eyes, spread her arms, and let herself fall backward. He caught her with ease and lowered her to the ground gently, leaving her lying flat on her back on the thick, green grass.

On his hands and knees above her, Trevor's heart caught in his throat. He didn't think the exercise was supposed to turn out this way, but with her lying on the ground, almost helpless beneath him, he wanted to scoop her up and kiss her.

Before he could make sense of the misfiring in his brain, she scrambled to her feet. Turning, she brushed the back of her pants free of a few blades of loose grass, then looked down at him. "Okay. Your turn."

He pushed his errant thoughts to the back of his mind, stood, closed his eyes, and extended his arms to the sides, just as she had. "You ready?" he asked.

"I'm ready, but are you sure you want to do this? You're a lot bigger than I am."

Trevor smiled, not opening his eyes. It was true—he stood taller than Janice by ten inches, and he surely outweighed her by sixty pounds. "I'm fine. With that red belt and all your martial arts training, you have to be stronger than you look. Here I come."

Without another word, Trevor let himself fall backward. Sure enough, both her arms slid under his arms and around his chest, cradling him as he came down. He let himself remain completely limp as she lowered him to the ground, although he felt himself slipping down much faster than he'd let her down.

With the speed at which the whole transaction occurred, she didn't pull one of her arms out from behind him quite fast enough. He landed on the ground with her wrist trapped beneath his shoulder blade and her forearm resting behind his neck, effectively pinning her so she was positioned almost on top of him.

In the position they were in, it would have taken no effort at all for him to wrap his arms around her, pull her down the last six inches between them, and kiss her. With very little effort, he could have embraced her with both arms and rolled over, pinning her on the ground beneath him, where he could have kissed her well and good.

But the whole exercise was a lesson in trust. If he did such a thing, she would never trust him again.

He ached inside with the loss, but lying flat on his back, Trevor twisted to raise his right shoulder off the ground to allow her to pull her arm out from beneath him, which she did.

He now understood that the silly exercise was a lesson in trust in more ways than he'd originally thought.

"You okay?" he asked as he stood.

"I'm fine," she mumbled, but Trevor was sure he heard a tremor in her voice that indicated she wasn't.

Now he was more certain than ever that they had to do the second half of the assignment.

With a quick swipe, he brushed a few pieces of grass from

his backside and off the backs of his legs. "Let's discuss the rest of the lesson as we walk. You haven't read it, so how would you like to read it out loud as we walk, and you can refresh my memory."

"Okay."

As they walked, she read a short paragraph about trusting your partner with your heart as well as your body. "The assignment is to tell your partner something either you've never told anyone before, a deep secret, or something you're too scared to tell anyone else. Something no one else knows. And you have to be able to trust the other person, first, to keep your secret, and second, not to use it against you." She kept her face facing forward as she walked, focusing only on the path straight ahead. "Do we really have to do this?"

He lowered his voice, although he didn't know why, because they were alone in that section of the park as they made their way to the ocean shoreline. "Yes. I think we should." His next words were almost painful. "Unless you don't trust me. It's okay if you don't. After all, we haven't known each other very long."

They arrived at the shoreline, but instead of stopping and sitting on the bench like he'd originally planned, they turned and began walking slowly on the seawall walkway.

"But I do trust you, strange as that sounds. I don't know why, but I do. I just don't know if you want to hear my silly problems."

She didn't stop walking, so neither did he. "I do want to hear them. I think trust goes hand in hand with honesty, so I'm going to be honest with you. When you told me about that self-defense class you've been taking, I wondered why you would take such a thing. Not that it's unusual for a woman to take such a course. I think that's a great idea. But when women take self-defense classes, most take a short thing that teaches a few basic self-defense moves, and then they carry bear spray and stay away from dark places at night. You've gone way beyond that. You've been doing this for years, and you're good enough to flatten a man with your bare hands. I want to know what happened to you that made you go to such extremes. I'm going to be honest with you and tell you that I've already asked Laura what happened, but she told me she doesn't know. She only told me that one night you came home really scared, and the next day you signed up for that martial arts thing and haven't looked back."

She remained silent as they walked. Trevor held his questions, knowing she needed the time to think and trusting that if she wanted to tell him, she would. If not, he would have to live with not knowing.

When she wrapped her arms around herself as they continued on, Trevor didn't think that was a good sign. Still, he waited for her to have the first word, even if she didn't speak until they finished their walk and returned to the car.

Her voice came out so soft he barely heard her over the pounding of the ocean waves on the sand.

"I haven't really talked to Laura about it. I don't know why. I guess I felt too stupid, like it was my own fault. I know that's dumb. It's never the victim's fault."

A lump went to war with the good meal he'd just eaten. Now he hated himself for what he had started. He didn't want to hear what he suspected was true, but at the same time, he had to know if she had been a victim of a brutal attack, or worse. . . . He found he couldn't speak, so he waited for her to continue.

"Don't worry. I'm not going to break down and cry on you. I'm okay."

He found it difficult to keep walking. He slowed to see if she would also slow and maybe stop, but she didn't. Therefore, he continued to walk. "Are you sure? It's okay if you're not."

"But I am okay. I wasn't hurt or anything, if that's what you're thinking. I was just scared. More scared than I'd ever been in my life. If it hadn't been for God's timing, though, I don't even want to think about what would have happened."

"Do you want to tell me? You don't have to."

Janice kept her focus straight ahead and continued to walk

with her arms wrapped around herself. "There's not a lot to tell. I had to work late one night. I missed the bus, so I decided to walk to another bus stop to take an alternate route. That ended up being a bad decision because on the way to the bus stop a couple of guys jumped me. At first they only wanted my money, but when they so easily overpowered me, I think they got different ideas. They dragged me between two buildings, but a police officer happened to be driving by and saw my purse lying on the ground. He stopped the cruiser, turned on the flashing red and blue lights, and then the two men dropped me and ran. I couldn't identify them, so they were never caught. But I truly believe that God sent that cop there at the right time. There was no other reason for him to notice my purse on the ground on a dark street. That's about it."

"Are you sure you weren't hurt?"

"Positive. Please don't worry about me. And don't ever believe it when someone tells you there's never a cop around when you need one. He also gave me the card for the martial arts studio I go to."

Trevor tried to tamp down a growing anger. "And you still take the bus back and forth to work every day? After what nearly happened?"

Suddenly, she stopped. Since he hadn't expected it, Trevor stopped three steps ahead of her, turned, and walked back, resulting in speaking to her face-to-face.

She unwrapped her arms from her waist and crossed them over her chest as she glared up at him. "I'm not going to live in fear for the rest of my life. I'm going to continue on as normal, a little more careful, and a little more prepared. Besides, cars sometimes break down, you know. For your information, I did take my car for awhile, until I figured I could take care of myself if anything like that happened again. I'm also much more careful around strangers. For awhile, I was afraid of everything, that someone would jump me from around every corner. Do you know what it's like to walk around like that, always being afraid? It's awful. I won't live like that again."

Being male and six feet tall, Trevor figured that even though he was sometimes nervous out at night in a strange area in a rougher end of town, he would never truly know the fear women faced when out alone, where danger could lurk around every corner. Also, he knew that in actual fact cases of women being attacked by a stranger were rare. More women were hurt by men they already knew, which only made it worse, because they didn't know who to trust. He couldn't imagine the trauma she'd experienced while working through the horror of being attacked and all the complications that went with it.

He didn't know what to say, so he said nothing.

She turned and smiled at him. "So, now it's your turn. What are you going to tell me about yourself that no one else knows?"

twelve

Janice turned around and started walking back to where they came from, trusting that Trevor's secret would take the same amount of time to share as hers. He quickly caught up with her, and they walked side by side in silence.

She still couldn't believe she actually told him. She hadn't told anyone, not even Laura, her best friend, how much that one incident had affected her. Until a few minutes ago, she hadn't realized herself how much it had affected her whole life, even after all this time.

While men who knew nothing of martial arts did come into the class as volunteers so the students could test their skills on someone besides their teacher, she'd never been able to truly use her skills outside the studio. More importantly, she'd never put her confidence to the test.

Today, when Trevor had unwittingly trapped her she knew beyond a shadow of doubt that she could have escaped if she had wanted to. If it hadn't been Trevor, she could have and would have done what she needed to do to be safe. Because it would have meant hurting Trevor, she hadn't reacted. But the important thing was that she knew she could have and would have, if necessary.

Nothing had happened, but in the event itself a question had been answered.

She had finally conquered her fear, fully and completely. She would never stop being sensible and careful, but from that moment on, she knew she would never have to walk in fear again. "Come on, Trevor. Being able to share that with you lifted a great weight off my shoulders. I never would have thought it would feel so good to tell you, and now I don't have to carry it alone. You can tell me something close to your

137

heart. Let me help you carry your burdens."

His voice dropped to a gravelly whisper. "I have to admit that a few people already know this. My parents and my doctor, but no one else. Not even Frank."

Something inside Janice went numb when he said "doctor." If something was seriously wrong with him, she thought she just might die inside. In everything they'd done together, he'd seemed healthy and fit. From his dietary habits, she knew he wasn't diabetic. However, being diabetic or anything like that was nothing anyone needed to keep secret. In her mind, she conjured up all the things that could be wrong with a person when they appeared normal on the outside but would be fatal in time.

All she could do was wait for him to tell her in his own time.

They walked in silence for a couple of minutes before he finally spoke. "I'm dyslexic."

She turned her head to study him as they walked, but his attention strayed everywhere except to her.

"I don't know much about dyslexia, only that it's some kind of learning disability that involves mixing up letters and things."

"Well, sometimes it's kind of like that, but not always, and there's more to it than that. It's a neurological dysfunction. All my life I've struggled with reading. I did graduate from high school, but I had to work very hard, and I didn't do very well. It still affects me, but it's not as bad as it used to be. I think I can safely say that I'm never going to go to a university and get a degree in anything. I'll probably be the maintenance guy for V. L. Management all my life."

She tried to encourage him with a smile, but she had a feeling he knew her smile was forced. "I much prefer your official title of Mechanical Engineer. Not everyone goes to the university. I'll probably never go either. I like my office job."

He turned to her. "I like my job too, but no one is ever going to talk about you behind your back and say you're stupid."

"But you're not stupid! I've also seen you read. You haven't had any difficulty with the lessons at the couples' counseling classes."

"That's different. Those aren't real books. And remember, much of the lesson assignments are read out loud during class. I don't have any trouble with oral instruction or problem solving when it's spoken, just when it's written down. It's hard to explain. I still read the occasional novel, and of course I read my Bible every day. But reading takes me longer than anyone else, and sometimes I don't understand what I read so easily. It's not always consistent, and some days are better than others. I don't have any trouble with anything else, just reading. I'm only a mild case, but it's there, and it will always be there. I've actually got a better memory than most people, and maybe that's why. You'll never believe what a relief it was when my parents had me tested and we had an explanation for it. We never told any of my teachers because my doctor told my parents that if I worked hard, I could probably pass on my own. Back in school I developed the most amazing ways to hide it, and I suppose I still do. Otherwise, I risked being treated differently than the rest of the kids. So instead of being labeled as mentally deficient, I was just labeled as lazy and a problem child. Praise God, my parents knew how hard I worked. They helped me as best they could and stuck up for me when I needed it."

"What about your sisters?"

"Statistically, it affects boys three to six times more often than girls. My sisters are fine."

"Is it genetic?"

"No one else in my family seems to have it, but who knows about past generations when they didn't have a name for it. Anyway, God loves me, I'm happy with my life, I have good friends and a good job I enjoy, so it really doesn't matter anymore."

She doubted that it didn't matter to him, especially if he'd never told anyone about it, not even Frank. Right then, Janice didn't care that she had to get up early for work. Tonight, before bed, she would do some significant searching on the Internet for more information on dyslexia.

He stopped and pointed to the ocean. "The sun is setting. Want to stand on the shore for awhile and watch?"

"Yes, I'd like that."

She stood at his side to watch the sky brighten with the pinks and purples of the spring sunset reflecting over the crystal surface of the endless ocean. With the fading light, the temperature continued to drop quickly. Even in her jacket, Janice couldn't suppress a shiver.

"Cold? Want to go?"

She wrapped her arms around herself. "No. Not yet."

Slowly, Trevor's arm wrapped around her shoulder, and he pulled her in close to him. "Better?"

It was better, not just for the warmth. The tender but firm way he cradled her spoke volumes—he didn't think less of her for her weaknesses, and the reassurance touched her deeply. She wished that she could somehow do the same for him.

The more she thought about his disability, the more she respected him. Even though he admitted to struggling at times, he *had* made a good life for himself. After more than two months of seeing him nearly every day, she still would never have guessed he had a learning disability. With his quick wit and eye for detail, she didn't know how anyone could ever perceive him as stupid. She would never have known he had a problem if he hadn't told her. She couldn't imagine the challenges he had overcome growing up.

To be trusted with such a painful and personal secret was a staggering responsibility and a vivid statement of how much he really did trust her, not just for the sake of the assignment, but for all time.

When the sun sank below the distant shore, leaving only a dull red glow in its wake, Janice turned her head to speak to Trevor. "I've had a lovely evening, but I guess it's time to go home."

"Yes. Tomorrow night is the class. How would you like to

join me for lunch? I can pick you up."

Janice smiled. He'd joined her for lunch many times in the last two months, and she'd enjoyed it every time. "I'd like that very much."

Just like every other time he announced he would be joining her, she could hardly wait.

ॐ

"Well? What do you think?"

Janice lowered her chin while she studied the fabric, trying to gauge if the green color suited her or not.

She heard Trevor clearing his throat. "I think it makes her look short."

Janice pushed the shiny fabric away and glared at him. She'd teased him about so many things she could no longer be angry with him for teasing her about her height. "How can a length of fabric make me look short? You're just saying that because you're mad that you had to come."

He leaned back in the chair, stretched his long legs out in front of him, crossed his ankles, then lifted his arms and linked his fingers behind his head. Those adorable little crinkles appeared at the corners of his striking blue eyes as he grinned. "I dunno. I can't think of a more manly place to hang out than the local fabric store. How about you, Frank? Are you having fun yet?"

"Oh, sure," Frank grumbled as he hunched in the chair, trying to hide so anyone walking by wouldn't see him through the store's large window.

Janice picked up the dress pattern and studied the picture. Having both the men's shirts and the maid of honor's dress made of the same fabric would look sharp, but she couldn't see it happening. "I can't believe you've left these things for the last minute like this. I know you've already altered your mother's wedding dress, but how are you going to make the two shirts and a dress for me in three weeks?"

Laura crossed her arms. "I can do a shirt in one day and the dress in two. There's lots of time."

Trevor held up a bag to shield himself as he spoke. "We have to make sure the photographer gets lots of pictures. Janice in a dress, especially a fancy dress, is going to be the eighth wonder of the modern world, and we're all going to be there when it happens."

Janice thumped the pattern on the top of the cabinet. "How dare you! I wore a dress a number of times when we went out. I've also been to your church a few times, and I wore a dress every time."

"That was a jean skirt you wore every time, not a dress. Doesn't count."

"Children! Stop fighting!" Laura interjected as she wrapped the fabric back around the bolt. "After we pay for this, Janice and I are going to go down the mall to pick up the napkins and stuff, and you guys have to go reserve your tuxes."

Trevor and Frank wasted no time in leaving the fabric store, so Janice helped Laura gather everything she needed for her rush sewing project and proceeded to the cutting table.

It was the opportunity Janice needed. She stood close to Laura while they waited their turn in the checkout line. "We always seem to be together with the guys, and then when we finally get home it's so late we hurry off to bed. I can't remember the last time we sat and talked, just the two of us."

"I know," Laura mumbled as she ran her finger down the notions list of the pattern, checking one last time that she had everything she needed. "I guess with the wedding approaching, everything we've done has been centered on getting ready for that."

"I was thinking, have you ever wondered if you're doing the right thing? There's only a few sessions left of that couples' counseling course, and I've sure gotten to know a different side of Trevor. Surely you must be seeing Frank in a different light since the whole thing started."

Laura simply shrugged her shoulders. "Not really. Some stuff, I guess. But not a lot."

Janice gritted her teeth, then turned to smile at Laura. "But what about when the topic of the week was romance versus routine? What it's like to really live with someone after the glow of the initial romance is over? The day-to-day stuff of living together and getting along when neither of you is at your best? When you no longer try to impress and when your partner no longer cares about impressing you? Do you really think you and Frank can be happy together?"

Laura shrugged her shoulders again. "Sure. Why not?"

Janice felt like dragging her hand down her face but restrained herself. While she struggled to think of the right thing to say, Laura raised her hand and rested it on Janice's shoulder. "You're not having problems with Trevor, are you?"

Janice blinked. "Problems with Trevor? No, there's nothing wrong between me and Trevor. But since the course began, we've gotten to know each other much better."

Janice had come to learn a lot about Trevor that no one else knew. She'd learned a lot about his dyslexia, and he'd told her what it was like to grow up with it. The whole time he'd been adamant about her not feeling sorry for him. They'd both found it funny that Janice hadn't wanted him to feel sorry for her due to her long-standing and recently resolved paranoias and fears about being out at night. He'd even agreed to be the aggressive male at one of her self-defense classes, risking his healthy male ego by getting beat up by a bunch of women.

In many ways, she now knew him better than Laura, who had been her best friend since elementary school. Likewise, she'd opened herself to Trevor completely, holding nothing back, even sharing many things she'd never told Laura. And he still liked her anyway.

"I guess the same thing has happened with me and Frank, now that I think about it. We've learned a lot about each other we didn't know, but nothing has changed."

Janice couldn't say the same. Everything had changed. Originally, she and Trevor had planned not to see each other again unless their paths crossed after Frank and Laura either split up or got married. Both of them had expressed regret that everything would soon be over and they wouldn't need to see each other every day. In doing so, they discussed the direction their friendship had taken and decided not only to keep in touch but to continue in their friendship as they were doing, just not every day.

Laura and Janice's turn to pay came before she could resume the conversation, so Janice had to tell herself that she'd planted a sufficient seed for the day and leave it in God's hands. She knew Trevor had experienced many of these same frustrations with Frank and suspected he was having another one at this same moment.

The girls couldn't see Frank and Trevor waiting for them when they walked out into the mall, so they headed for the men's shop to meet them.

"Janice?"

Janice turned at the sound of a male voice that sounded only slightly familiar.

"Rick! I haven't seen you for a long time. How are you?" She quickly glanced over his shoulder to see if Sarah was with him, but she wasn't.

"I'm doing fine. I see that blond guy isn't with you. Dan told me you were going to that couples' thing Pastor Harry is doing. I see you're not officially engaged yet, and the class is almost over. I was wondering if anything has changed?"

"Well, actually—" A squeak escaped her mouth as an arm slid around her waist.

"Hi. Rick, is it? If I'm the blond guy you're referring to, the name is Trevor."

Rick's ears reddened. "Hi, Trevor. I didn't see you."

Trevor's one arm tightened around her waist, pulling her in closer to him. He extended his free hand to Rick.

As Rick grasped Trevor's hand, Trevor lowered his chin, drawing particular attention to the fact that he stood three inches taller than Rick. He met Rick's gaze with a stony stare. "Yeah. I can see how I'd be hard to miss."

Very slowly, their hands moved up and down in a brief

handshake. By Rick's slight wince, Janice could tell that Trevor was squeezing a little too hard. When Trevor finally released Rick's hand, Rick backed up a step and flexed his fingers at his side.

One corner of Trevor's mouth quirked up. "Maybe I'll catch you some Sunday at church, Rick. You'll probably be seeing me there more often. Just look for Janice, and I'll be there."

"Uh, yeah. Well, it was nice meeting you again, Trevor. See you, Janice." Rick turned and walked away. Frank, Trevor, and Laura stood in silence, watching Rick go. Janice watched Trevor. His mouth was set in a grim line, and his eyes narrowed as he glared at Rick's diminishing form.

Laura glanced at Janice, then turned and tugged on Frank's sleeve. "There's something I want to show you. Over there."

Without another word, Frank and Laura disappeared into the bakery a few doors down.

Janice pulled out of Trevor's grasp. She crossed her arms and tapped one foot, the sound echoing on the floor. "That was rather immature, don't you think?"

Trevor crossed his arms as he continued to watch Rick walk down to the end of the mall. "He annoys me."

"That was no reason to be rude."

"I wasn't rude. Name one thing I said that was rude."

"You know what I mean."

Trevor turned to face her. He rested one fist on his hip and jerked his other thumb over his shoulder in the direction Rick had gone. "He had no right to ask you if I'm past news. None. Not while we're still taking that course together."

Janice blinked and stared. If it had been anyone else, she would have said he was jealous. But this was Trevor. Her friend. They were pretending to be a couple only because they had a specific purpose in mind. They both knew that.

"And another thing. He knew my name perfectly well. We were introduced before, and I remembered his name just fine, especially considering the circumstances of our original meeting. He was just trying to diminish my position as your official boyfriend by calling me 'that blond guy.' "

"You're taking this awful personal, Trevor."

"That's because it *is* personal."

Janice dearly wished she could have asked him why, but Frank and Laura returned, cutting their conversation short.

Together, they browsed through a few more stores, bought the supplies to decorate the hall and tables at the wedding, and then went home.

Since they had gone out as two couples most evenings, they had developed a pattern to allow themselves a minute of privacy from each other as they parted. Since it was Frank's car, Frank and Laura stayed at the car to say their good-byes, and Trevor escorted Janice to the door of the house.

She didn't want to spoil the evening, so Janice decided not to question him further about the incident with Rick. However, when this whole thing was over, she knew she would have to seek Rick out and talk to him, because now the same thing had happened twice.

Standing nearly toe-to-toe, Trevor grasped both of her hands between them, as he often did. "I can't remember whose church we're going to tomorrow. I guess yours, since there's only two Sundays left before the wedding."

"That's right."

"Okay. I'll see you tomorrow."

He released her hands but didn't back away. Instead, he shuffled closer and cupped her chin with both hands. His voice dropped to a low, husky whisper. "Good night, Janice."

His head lowered.

Janice's heart stopped beating.

His eyes closed.

Her heart started pounding in double-time.

Janice tipped her chin up without his prompting.

His lips touched hers softly, barely touching, then lifted. Before the disappointment fully sank in, his hands drifted to her back, his mouth settled in for a full contact, and he kissed her for real.

Janice couldn't do anything else. She reached around his back to embrace him and returned his kiss.

Too soon, he released her mouth and stepped away. His hands drifted from her back and grasped her hands between them once again, as he should have in the first place.

Janice cleared her throat. "What was that for?"

"I don't know. I guess I like you. Isn't that a good enough reason?"

"I thought we were supposed to be just friends. Friends don't do that."

"Then maybe we should be special friends."

Janice shook her head. "No. I've heard that a romance that isn't meant to be will destroy a friendship. I value what we have too much to risk ruining it. I want to stay just plain old friends and nothing more."

"Are you sure?"

She had to force the words out. "Yes, I'm sure. I've never been more sure of anything in my life. What we have is good and unique, and I want to keep it that way."

A long silence loomed between them.

She couldn't have it any other way. The fear that gripped her soul over the thought of something going wrong terrified her unlike anything she'd ever experienced. Trevor was the sweetest man she'd ever known. His gentleness when she needed it only emphasized his strength where it counted. They could share anything and everything—and did. She'd never known anyone like him and knew she never would again. What they had between them was too valuable to do anything to risk it.

She had to keep him as her friend forever.

"If that's the way you think it should be, then that's the way it is. Besides church tomorrow, do we have anything else planned with Frank and Laura?"

She'd never been so grateful for a change in subject, but she had a feeling Trevor had done it on purpose. "Yes. Dinner on Monday. Tuesday and Wednesday Laura's going to sew

Frank's and your shirts. Thursday you guys are coming here for dinner to try on the shirts and then we're doing more shopping. Then Friday is the last class."

"That means we're almost out of time. Do you think this wedding is really meant to happen?"

She shrugged her shoulders. "I don't know. We should really get together some time without Frank and Laura and pray about it some more."

He nodded. "I'll call you at lunchtime Monday, and we'll set something up without those two listening in. In the meantime, I'll see you tomorrow."

thirteen

"Welcome to week eleven of our Getting To Know You, Spring Session. This is our last class together as a group. For next week we'll have individual sessions for every couple. There's a sign-up sheet in the back. If you don't see anything suitable, please speak to me privately after class.

"Last week we talked about conflict and resolution. Today we're going to be talking about the causes of successes and failures in a marriage. Brittany, can you hand out one of these booklets to everyone, please?"

As he accepted a booklet, Trevor glanced at Frank and Laura. This was it, the last session of the class that was supposed to help Frank and Laura get to know each other beyond the smiles and warm fuzzies. Even after all that had been discussed and all the weekly assignments, Frank and Laura openly held hands and gazed at each other with such starstruck expressions that Trevor thought he might be sick. Over the past four months, he and Janice had become even more convinced than when the whole fiasco started and they first began their quest of how ill-suited Frank and Laura were for each other. If it wasn't his imagination, he also had the impression a few others in their group also thought the same way.

When everyone had opened the newest booklet to the first page, Pastor Harry began.

"Experience has taught me that one of the major causes of the breakdown of a marriage or any kind of relationship is the lack of effective communication. How do you communicate with your partner?"

He paused to let his statement sink in around the room.

Trevor bit back a smirk. Since Frank and Laura announced their engagement, he'd seen Janice almost every day. When together, they tended to talk a lot. In those days they hadn't been with each other in person, they somehow usually ended up spending a fair amount of time on the phone. Most of the time he called her, but sometimes she phoned him. The conversations always started the same, clarifying upcoming plans to be with Frank and Laura. Then they always seemed to drift onto something totally unrelated to the original topic. A number of times they'd talked so long that Frank gave up and went to bed, then yelled at him to shut up so he could sleep.

He hadn't spent as much time on the phone in the past four years as he had in the past four months. In that short space of time, he'd come to know Janice better than Frank, his best friend whom he'd known all his life.

The sensation of being poked in the ribs brought his thoughts back to the class.

"Pay attention!" Janice whispered through her teeth. "This is about communication, and you're sitting there daydreaming."

Trevor turned to Janice and grinned at her like a Cheshire cat, showing all his teeth. She made a disgusted grunt, then turned to watch Pastor Harry as he continued to talk.

Of course, Trevor agreed with everything the pastor said, especially when the topic centered around disagreements and arguments. He'd never seen Frank and Laura have a single disagreement, which made him doubt they were communicating effectively. However, he'd had a few humdingers with Janice.

When she was mad at him, she let him have it right between the eyes. There was no guessing that she was angry, nor did he ever have to guess at why. He simply knew it. He also liked it that way. They could deal with the problem, and life went on as usual.

So far, Janice had done nothing to make him angry, so he wasn't quite sure what would happen in that case. However, that was no surprise. All his life, Trevor tended to be even-tempered, and he didn't become angry often. He also tried to act intelligently when he was angry. Instead of roaring off in his car or punching holes in the walls like some of the men he knew, he went for a walk until he calmed down and could think rationally.

The pastor's words interrupted his thoughts. "I'll give you ten minutes to answer the questions, then ten minutes to talk about your answers between yourselves. Then we'll open up for sharing before we go on to the next chapter."

He started scribbling down his answers. In the middle of question three, Janice poked him again.

"What?" he muttered as he tried to complete his sentence.

"I have to go," she whispered.

Trevor raised his head and glanced toward the door. He could never figure out why women couldn't go to the washroom alone when in a crowded room or restaurant. "So? Go. You don't need me to hold your hand if Laura's busy."

"I meant leave. I have to go home. Now."

The pen froze in the middle of a word. "Now? Is something wrong? Are you all right?" He narrowed his eyes and studied her face.

"No, I'm not all right. In twenty minutes, I'm going to be sick. I've got just enough time if we leave right now."

He laid the pen in his lap. "I've never seen someone be sick on a stopwatch before. What's really wrong?"

She lowered her head and pressed the fingertips of both hands to her temples. "I just saw a flash of light, and I'm getting a really bad headache, very fast. That means I'm getting a migraine. I have to lie down in the dark, and if I can do it fast enough, maybe I won't be sick. But since I'm out and can't go straight to bed, it's going to be too late to ward off the progression. Within twenty minutes, I'm going to be throwing up."

Trevor had never had a migraine in his life, but he'd heard they were awful.

He turned to Frank. "We've got to go. Now."

Frank laid his pen down and glanced up at the clock on the wall. "What are you talking about? Class just started."

Still sitting, Trevor bent at the waist and leaned closer to

Frank so those around him wouldn't overhear. "Janice is getting a migraine."

Laura leaned closer and covered her mouth with both hands. "Oh, no," she said from between her fingers. "You've got to get her home right away." She reached into her purse for her keys, then froze. "I forget. How did we get here? We didn't take my car this time, did we?"

"I drove this time," Trevor said. "You've either got to come with me right now or find someone else to drive you back."

Glancing out the corner of his eye, he saw Janice get up and leave. He wanted to call out to her that he'd be there in a minute, but he didn't want to disturb the class any more than he was already doing. He also didn't know the severity of her headache, so he didn't want to make any sharp or sudden noises.

He turned back to Frank. "Make up your mind. You have fifteen seconds, then I'm leaving whether you're with me or not."

Pastor Harry watched the door close behind Janice as she went outside. "Excuse me. Is something wrong?"

Trevor glanced around the room. Everyone was staring at him. He tried to smile to everyone but failed.

He stood. "Janice doesn't feel well, and we've got to go. Can someone give Frank and Laura a ride home? Otherwise, they've got to come with me."

"I can drive them home," Pastor Harry said. "Give Janice my best, and we'll all pray for her."

At the pastor's words, Trevor darted across the room. He opened the door and let it slam behind him as he increased his speed and ran as fast as he could to the car.

He unlocked the car door and stepped aside. As Janice slid in slowly, his stomach did another flip-flop. In only a few minutes, the pallor of her skin had become alarming.

They both remained completely silent as he drove as fast as he could back to her house, trying his best not to make sudden movements or get a speeding ticket. They arrived in thirteen minutes. Counting the three minutes it took to get moving in the first place, that meant she had four minutes of grace.

He watched her hand shake as she fumbled with the key in the lock. Without asking for her permission, he removed the key chain from her hand and opened the door.

She didn't say a word as she hurried through the house and into her bedroom, her head down and her fingertips pressed to her temples.

Trevor remained standing in the living room. The bedsprings creaked, and then, except for the hum of the fridge, all was silent.

He didn't know what to do. He thought he could remember something about a cold facecloth helping in a case like this, but he wasn't sure.

Since it couldn't hurt, Trevor walked into the hallway to the linen closet. The second he touched the knob to pull the bifold door open, the bedsprings creaked again. Janice stepped out of the bedroom, one hand pressed to her temple, the other over her mouth. She ran all the way into the bathroom, and the door banged shut.

A soulful moan drifted through the closed door, and she started to retch.

Trevor thought he might be sick too.

He stood in the hall, his hand still on the linen closet doorknob. He couldn't just stand there and do nothing. She needed him.

He walked softly to the bathroom door and tested the doorknob. It turned, so he slowly pushed the door open. Janice was hunched over the toilet, one arm wrapped around her stomach, the other palm still pressed to her temple. Her complexion had faded to a ghastly pale gray. It also dawned on him that she wasn't wearing her glasses. He'd never seen her without her glasses before, not even the time they went swimming.

"Go away," she moaned. "You can go home now."

Trevor stepped beside her, hunkered down, and wrapped one arm around her waist. He could feel her trembling all over. In addition to her cheeks being without color, they were also wet with tears.

"Shh," he whispered. "I'm not going anywhere."

He expected her to tell him to leave, but before she could speak, she retched again.

Trevor did the only thing he could, and that was to hold her until she got everything out of her system, then he led her back to bed.

When she was lying down and still, Trevor walked across the room, trying to ignore the fact that he was in her bedroom. He closed the blinds to make it as dark as possible until the sun fully set. He remained beside the window and turned. "Would a cold facecloth help?"

She lay on the bed with her arm over her eyes, her whole body unnaturally still. Her voice came out in a low mumble, barely discernable. "There's an ice bag in the freezer."

Trevor tiptoed as fast as he could out of the bedroom and ran to the kitchen. He located a gel-style athletic ice bag, wrapped the dishtowel around it, and hurried back to the bedroom. When he stood beside the bed, Janice lifted her arm from her face and raised her hands to accept it from him. Tearstains lined her cheeks, and a few new tears trickled through her tightly-closed eyelids.

He felt like he'd been dealt a sucker punch to the gut.

Instead of handing her the ice bag, he gently placed it over her forehead for her, making sure the towel covered it properly.

"Is this right?" he whispered, barely able to choke the words out.

She pressed the ice bag down with her fingertips and spoke so softly he could barely hear her. "Yes. Thank you. You can go now."

He didn't go. He wanted to touch her, to gently smooth away the hair from her forehead. To brush away the wetness from her cheeks. To help reposition the ice bag to put the coldest part over her forehead. But he was too afraid.

Trevor rammed his hands into his pockets. "I'm not going anywhere," he whispered back, not knowing how loud he could speak, hoping she heard him. "What causes this?"

Her voice trembled when she spoke. "It doesn't happen that often, but there are some food triggers that I try to avoid. Chocolate is my weakness. I don't know what started it today. I've been so careful with what I've eaten."

Trevor shuffled his feet but otherwise didn't move. He stood beside the bed with his hands still deep in his pockets.

"Is there anything I can get for you? Some medicine or something? Do you take that kind of thing? I don't know what to do, but I'm not leaving you like this. At least not until Laura gets home."

"In the medicine cabinet. In the bathroom. It's the only prescription bottle with my name on it."

He returned in a minute flat, a pill in one hand, a glass of cool water in the other. Very carefully, he helped her sit up and supported her back while she swallowed the pill with a tiny sip of water. As gently as he could, he slowly lowered her back down. He let her adjust the ice bag on her forehead by herself, and then he stood beside the bed.

Another tear escaped her closed eyelids. She sniffled, then winced. "I didn't want you to see me like this," she mumbled.

This time, he couldn't help himself. She still wasn't wearing her glasses, and their absence made her seem totally vulnerable. With as soft a touch as he could manage, he brushed the errant lock of hair back from her forehead. "Don't worry about it. Now you be quiet and see if you can sleep."

Trevor stood and watched in silence for a full twenty minutes before her breathing slowed and became shallow and perfectly uniform. Even knowing she was sleeping, he couldn't leave her side.

This still, silent creature on the bed had last week threatened to flatten him in the middle of the parking lot after he'd teased her about something insignificant. And he had no doubt that she would have done it if he hadn't run, laughing, calling back to her that she couldn't hurt him if she couldn't catch him. Of course, she had been laughing too, which made it harder to take each other seriously.

Frank and Laura had watched them in total disgust. Trevor had never had so much fun in his life.

Janice now lay completely immobile. Defenseless. A wounded angel. And there was nothing he could do about it.

He'd never felt so helpless in his life.

As he continued to stand beside her still form, the revelation struck him. In some ways, it had happened so fast; but in another way, it snuck up on him slowly, a little bit each day, so gradually he didn't see it happening. But now he couldn't deny it. He hadn't known her long in the overall scheme of life, but since they started spending so much time together she'd become his very best friend in the whole world. Their relationship had gone far deeper than mere friendship. Trevor had totally and completely fallen in love.

The front door creaked open, and soft footsteps approached behind him.

"Is she sleeping?" Laura whispered.

"Yes," he whispered back.

"We should get out of here. Want some tea?"

He followed Laura out of the room. "No, thanks. I really should be going. Is she going to be okay tomorrow?"

"Usually she is, but that medication makes her real dozy. She's not going to be good for much until sometime in the afternoon. Good thing tomorrow's Saturday."

"I understand. Tell her to phone me when she's feeling better."

"You bet. Good night, Trevor."

≈

Trevor leaned his hip into the doorframe of Janice's kitchen. "How long do you think they'll be?"

She poured the water into the coffeemaker and turned around. "I'm figuring they'll be back in about an hour. That gives us just the right amount of time."

As he continued to prop himself against the doorway, Janice fidgeted with everything she laid her hands on, something she never did.

Tomorrow was Thursday, the wedding rehearsal, and then

two days after that, Saturday, the wedding. Frank and Laura had done their private appointment with Pastor Harry, and they were really going through with it. Trevor had a feeling he and Janice were going to pray about it one more time, talk, and then leave it in God's hands and let whatever happened, happen, just as they'd discussed and agreed a million times.

Such being the case, he didn't know why Janice seemed to be developing a case of the nervous jitters. She picked up and put down everything she could possibly touch until the coffee was ready.

When she poured the coffee into two waiting mugs, Trevor found the cream in the fridge and topped off both cups.

As soon as they sat on the couch and placed their hot mugs onto a magazine on the coffee table, Janice folded her hands in her lap and turned to face him.

"Before we pray together about Laura and Frank, there's something I have to say to you. It's about us."

Trevor's heart pounded. He crossed his arms over his chest, so she wouldn't be able to see his hands shaking.

He'd hoped and prayed for this moment, the moment she told him that she loved him as much as he'd come to love her. Since they'd already discussed so many times the what-ifs of Frank and Laura actually going through with the wedding, he had already prepared himself for whatever happened afterward. If they were happy together, he would praise God, and life would go on just fine. If Frank and Laura weren't happy together, Trevor would be the best friend he could be to Frank and help him through whatever life threw at him.

Either way, the wedding would be over, and he would be free from his agreement with Janice to pretend to be a couple.

The minute everything was over, he planned to tell Janice that he was through pretending. He wanted to make their relationship as a couple real. She had tried to feed him some song and dance about friendship and romance not being compatible, but Trevor didn't agree. If they tried dating and it didn't work, he would gladly go back to the friendship they had developed, but he wanted them to try. If it didn't work, even though it wouldn't be the ideal solution, he could love her from the distance of a safe, platonic friendship. But if it did work, he would be the happiest man on earth.

Janice leaned forward in her seat. "As you know, the wedding is in three days. It looks like everything we tried hasn't worked, and they're going through with it after all. I guess you know that after the wedding there will be no need for us to keep pretending as we have been."

Trevor bit his lip to stop himself from blurting out his feelings and to let her finish talking. "Yes, I know."

"I've thought long and hard about this, and I thought you should know what I've decided. I'm going to go talk to Rick."

Trevor knotted his brows. "Rick? What for?"

"First of all, I have to explain to him why you acted the way you did in front of Frank and Laura. I know he won't be angry, but I do feel I have to explain. And then, if he asks me out, which I think he's going to do, I'm going to say yes."

Trevor's whole body went numb. All his hopes and dreams came crashing down around him. "What? Why?"

"I'm getting too mixed up about what's happened with us. We've known each other such a short amount of time, and everything is happening so fast. I need some time, and I need to distance myself and sort everything out. Since we agreed to remain just friends, I think I should pursue other romantic relationships. If Rick is still interested, that allows me to sort myself out while I see where that leads."

Trevor jumped to his feet. "I don't understand. I thought we had something special between us. Why do you feel the need to see someone else?"

Janice remained seated. She looked up at him from her place on the couch as she spoke. "It's not that I feel a need to see anyone. I just feel really mixed up, and I need time to figure some stuff out."

The front door creaked open.

"We're ba–ack!" Laura singsonged.

"Hey, Buddy," Frank said as he approached the couch. "We gotta go. There's a problem with my cummerbund, and if they can't get it fixed, we have to pick new ones, which might mean some quick alterations. That means you would have to try it on. They close in twenty minutes. We have just enough time if we go now."

"But. . ." Trevor let his voice trail off as he turned to Janice. "We were talking about something important."

Janice stood and shook her head. "It's okay, Trevor. We can talk more about it tomorrow after the rehearsal. Go now."

Trevor stood and left. It was the hardest thing he'd ever had to do in his life.

fourteen

As the maid of honor, Janice walked up the aisle first, humming the wedding march to herself.

"Janice! Slow down!" Laura called from behind her. "It's a wedding, not a race!"

Janice slowed her step and continued to walk slowly, as she'd been told to do.

She couldn't believe this was really happening. It was Thursday, two days before the wedding. They were actually going through the rehearsal, and Frank and Laura really were getting married on Saturday. Most of the church had been decorated. They only had a few things left to do on Friday, and all arrangements were in place. It was really going to happen.

Neither she nor Trevor thought Laura and Frank were doing the right thing. So she and Trevor had found a little time before the practice started while everyone was doing the decorating and prayed together one last time, agreeing that they had left it in God's hands, and even though it wasn't what they wanted, it was done.

As she stepped to the side, she smiled weakly at Trevor, who was already standing beside Frank. They then waited for Laura and her father to position themselves and start their walk up the aisle.

While they worked on setting Laura's hand on the right place on her father's arm, Janice watched Trevor out the corner of her eye.

She wasn't looking forward to the wedding, but she sure did want to see Trevor in a tuxedo. She knew she was setting herself up for a disappointment by dreaming about Trevor in a tux. Rick would also be at the wedding, and she had decided not to waste any time and to talk to him right away. As difficult as it would be for her to see Trevor with another woman, she had to accept that as friends, and friends only, they both would have to watch each other date.

The thought stabbed her where she didn't think she'd heal. She really didn't want to date Rick, nor did she think she would survive watching Trevor date other women. However, since she didn't know what else to do to get on with their lives and remain friends, she couldn't see any other alternative.

Janice did her best to push those thoughts out of her head and tried to concentrate on going through the motions of practicing for the wedding ceremony.

After they were done, Pastor Harry took Laura's parents to the side and talked to them privately. Janice and Trevor joined Frank and Laura, who were pointing to the podium and the potted fern arranged in front of it.

"You know," Laura said, sighing as she spoke, "I can almost see Bunners peeking through the leaves and wiggling his cute little nose at me."

Frank groaned. "I can't believe you named a rabbit Bunners. I still don't know where we're going to put that dumb bunny, either. You better not let it run around loose because Freddie will be watching it. I don't want you to be mad at me if one day that thing is gone."

"Pardon me?" Laura squeaked.

"I usually feed Freddie rats I buy from the pet store, but when a snake gets that size, people often feed them rabbits."

Laura's face paled. "Then I think you should get rid of Freddie."

Frank's face hardened. "I'm not getting rid of Freddie. You should get rid of that rabbit."

"And while we're on the topic of getting rid of things, I don't like the way you seem to think that you can tell me to get rid of my stuff. My stuff is just as good as yours."

"Forget it, Laura. You're just tired. Actually, I'm tired too. Knock it off. Your constant whining is getting on my nerves."

"Constant whining? You're being unreasonable, which you are a lot of the time."

"I'm not unreasonable. You have your head in the clouds on a regular basis. I'm just trying to be practical."

"Practical?" Laura sputtered. "I'm not the one who thinks nothing of living on credit, then wonders why the only thing you can afford to eat for a week is macaroni and wieners."

"Laura, if there's one thing I'm going to do with you after we're married, it's going to be to teach you not to be so cheap."

"And I'm going to teach you how to be more sensitive. How dare you say that about me in front of my friends!"

Janice felt Trevor's hand on her forearm. "Uh-oh," he mumbled as he gently guided her back a few steps.

They stood back and watched as Frank and Laura began hurling insults at each other.

Frank stiffened from head to toe and crossed his arms over his chest as he spoke in low, harsh tones. Tears started to stream down Laura's cheeks, and her voice skipped as she responded.

The pastor stopped talking. He didn't move, but he did watch Frank and Laura as the argument escalated.

Janice felt more than saw Trevor lean down to whisper in her ear. "I don't think they're doing that right. The book says they should communicate effectively, but that's not doing it very constructively."

Janice nodded and said nothing as the conversation continued to deteriorate exponentially. Even though it was what she and Trevor had been striving for over the past four months, it gave her no joy to hear Frank and Laura tossing back and forth opposing personality traits and conflicting characteristics that weren't necessarily bad, just not compatible for a permanent relationship, especially when discussed in anger.

Suddenly, the room fell silent, except for the sound of Laura's sniffling.

Both Frank and Laura turned to their guests—the pastor, their parents, and to Janice and Trevor.

Laura swiped her arm across her face, but it was Frank who addressed everyone.

"I don't think Laura and I are going to get married after all." He swept one hand in the air to encompass the decorating. "I know everything has all been set up. We'll be back in a minute to decide what to do about it. For now, Laura and I have to go talk in private."

A stunned silence hung in the room as Frank and Laura walked out.

"Wow," Trevor muttered. "Who would have thought it would come to this?"

"Yeah," Janice mumbled. "This is what we wanted to happen. Why do I not feel very happy about it?'

"I know. It's like that old saying in reverse. We've been trying and trying to get them to see each other realistically all this time and couldn't get them to see it. Now they do. We lost every battle but won the war. Still, there is no victory here."

The backs of Janice's eyes burned, and her throat clogged up. Her eyes welled up, and a couple of tears escaped. "No, I don't feel particularly happy about this either. With the heartache to Frank and Laura, all this wedding stuff around us just seems to rub everyone's noses in it too. I know it's better in the long run, but it's awful to see it around me right now."

Trevor stepped in front of her. Very slowly, he brushed his thumbs up under her glasses and wiped the tears from beneath her eyes.

"You know, dating for a long time before getting married isn't what builds a good marriage. My Great-Grampa Elliott and Grammie Louise don't talk a lot about their courtship, but I do know that they didn't know each other very long before they got married, only a few months. The old codger is going to be eighty-eight this year, but you should see the old guy go, especially when Grammie calls him City Boy. I've been trying to get them to tell me the story of that for years, but all they do is laugh. My point, though, is that they've been happily married over sixty years after a very short courtship."

"I don't understand what you're trying to say. What does this have to do with Frank and Laura?"

"I wasn't thinking about them. I was thinking about us. How do you feel about me, Janice? Do you really want to stay friends and date guys like Rick? Or do you want to be with me every day, sharing what we know is good? Living together and spending the rest of our lives together, in friendship and in love."

"Living together?"

One corner of his mouth quirked up, and his voice dropped in pitch. "This is coming out all wrong. I love you, Janice. I don't know when I started loving you, but when we were going through the motions of the ceremony before Laura and Frank called it off, I found myself thinking about what it would be like if this were my wedding. Our wedding."

"Our wedding?"

"I guess I'm asking if you'll marry me."

Janice's heart stopped, then started up again in double-time. She did love him. Like Trevor, she didn't know either when she started loving him, but she couldn't bear the thought of them going their separate ways. The only reason she thought it would be a good idea to date others was to avoid a romance between them that might spoil their friendship. All last night she'd lain awake, thinking about Trevor and his reaction to her words.

Of course he was right. She wouldn't be able to watch him date other women when she loved him to the depths of her soul. Nor did she think he would be able to stand watching her date other men. Without words, she already knew he loved her; and she suspected he already knew she loved him, or he wouldn't have asked her to marry him.

"Of course I'll marry you. You knew before you asked."

"When? I don't want a long engagement, and we've already been through the premarital counseling thing."

"Yes, but we missed the last private session. We'll have to at least do that."

"Yes, we will." His hands slipped to the sides of her waist, and she put her hands on his. "Look at all this around us. Do you think our wedding will be anything like this?"

Janice thought about what was all around them—all of it going to waste. Everything was in place for a wedding that wasn't going to happen. The church was decorated, the minister present, the caterer booked, the limo reserved. . . Everything was ready, and it was too late to stop it.

"I suppose I'd do much the same. I even like Laura's green color scheme. I guess you and I are going to have to deal with everything tomorrow. I hope it's not too late, and they won't lose all their deposits. I know the one for the caterer was really big."

She heard as well as felt Trevor's sharp intake of breath. "Unless we use everything ourselves. What if *we* get married on Saturday?"

"Us? Just like that? I've never done anything impulsive in my life. I don't think this is a good time to start."

"Well, it's up to you, of course. All I know is that Laura's friends are your friends, and Frank's friends are my friends. Both sets of our parents are already coming. When our wedding comes, there will only be a few minor changes to the guest list. Not a single person I'd like to invite to my wedding who isn't already coming wouldn't drop everything and come with a day's notice. All it would take is a few phone calls. What about you?"

"I suppose. . . But what about the marriage license?"

"My cousin Benny works for city hall, and he's good friends with his supervisor. If we call him tonight, I'll bet he'd be happy to rush it through tomorrow so we could have it by Saturday afternoon."

"I don't know. . ."

She didn't want to rush such an important decision, but when she knew beyond a shadow of doubt that it was right, there was no need to wait.

Janice reached up to run one finger across the tip of Trevor's chin. The little gesture gave her goose bumps. "I can't make such a decision so fast. I think we should pray about it first, don't you?"

Keeping his hands on her waist, he lowered his head until their foreheads touched. "Dear heavenly Father, this day has taken such an unexpected turn of events, but yet I can see Your hand in it as for the best for Frank and Laura. I now ask for Your guidance and Your wisdom in the decision Janice and I now face."

Janice softly cleared her throat. "Father, I'm not impulsive. Deep in my heart, I do want to marry Trevor, and I do want to marry him right away. But Your will is not always the same as our will. I'm scared to be heading into such a life-changing decision so fast. I too ask for Your wisdom and guidance and for confirmation that this would be the right thing. Please help us make this decision. I ask this in the name of our Lord and Savior, Jesus Christ, amen."

They both sighed deeply and released each other.

"So now what?" Trevor asked.

Before she could reply, Pastor Harry joined them.

"I hate to see it end like this for Frank and Laura. To be honest, I've had my doubts about them all along. Not that this makes me happy, but I firmly believe that their decision was for the best. As a pastor, I've seen a few weddings canceled but never at the last minute like this. I look around and see everything is ready to happen, but with no bride and groom, the wedding's off. By the way, what about you two? We never had that last appointment to discuss your wedding. Have you set a date yet? Because I can hardly wait to see you two married. It's been a pleasure to have a couple like you with such a solid relationship and strong potential for a great future together in my class."

Trevor smiled at Janice so sweetly she thought she might melt. All she could do was smile and nod.

"What about your dress?" he asked. "You can't get married in a green dress."

"That's okay. I'll just wear my jeans because they're blue. I have a white blouse and white sneakers."

"I don't think so," he grumbled. "I've heard that wedding ditty about something borrowed and something blue often enough in the past month. There's no way jeans legally count as the blue thing. I don't care if you wear your sneakers underneath whatever you wear, but can't you borrow a real wedding dress? What about your mother's dress? You said you're short like her. Has she still got it? I hear women tend to keep those things. Or can't you just buy a dress off the rack tomorrow? They have things like that, don't they?"

Janice couldn't tamp down her smile. "I was planning on wearing my mother's dress when I get married because it was her mother's dress too. I don't expect Laura to start sewing for me, considering what happened, but my mother sews. I'll bet she could do any alterations that need doing in one day. I wouldn't think there's much to be done."

His arms circled her waist, and he broke out into a wide smile. The adorable little crinkles at the corners of his beautiful blue eyes had never looked so wonderful.

Slowly, his smile faded, and his mouth opened like he was going to say something, but no words came out. Instead he smiled again, bent down, and brushed a slow, gentle kiss to her lips.

When they separated, he spoke to Pastor Harry but kept his eyes fixed on hers. "There's a different bride and groom and a few changes to the seating arrangements, but you're wrong, Pastor. The wedding's on."

epilogue

Trevor turned the doorknob slowly so Janice wouldn't hear him coming in. With as much stealth as he could muster, he poked his head in to first determine where she was.

Clunking noises echoed from the kitchen. Trevor closed the door slowly behind him and tiptoed inside with his hands behind his back.

"Honey, I'm ho–ome!" he chorused as he rounded the corner.

Janice squealed. She turned around in a flash at the same time as she whipped something behind her back.

Trevor grinned. He could see she hadn't forgotten either.

He brought out the flowering hibiscus plant from behind his back.

She didn't bring forward whatever she was hiding behind her back. "What are you doing home so soon?" she squeaked. "And what is that for?"

Trevor sighed. Maybe she had forgotten. "Today is our anniversary, remember? Flowers are supposed to be a sign of affection, and this is something that won't die after a few days, so you can be reminded every day of how much I love you."

"Oh, brother," she mumbled. "Like I need a reminder." Instead of bringing out whatever she was hiding from him, she quickly glanced at the back door, then back to him. "You're home early. I wasn't expecting you so soon."

He cleared his throat. "I have to admit the plant wasn't my first thought. I've been checking every couple of days for a suitable dog to rescue, and today they got one in that sounded so perfect. I got off early to go to the pound and see him. If he was right, I was going to bring him home for you. But when I got there, someone else had got there first. I just thought that it would have been a nice anniversary surprise. I guess we'll have to wait."

He leaned toward her to give her a kiss, but she turned her head, only allowing him to kiss her cheek.

"Why do you keep looking into the backyard? And what's that strange noise?"

Suddenly, the door thumped. Trevor plunked the plant on the counter and ran to the back door.

"Trevor! Wait!"

He opened the door. As he looked into the yard, something bumped into his leg. He looked down in time to see a blur scoot past his feet. As Janice squatted down, she dropped a blue dog bowl on the floor and scooped up a rather matted, little, hairy brown dog.

Trevor's throat clogged. Words failed him.

Janice stood with the dog in her arms. "I can't believe this. After we talked about it, I've been checking at the pound every couple of days too. It looks like I was the one who beat you to him. I was going to bathe him and try and do something with his coat before you saw him. He doesn't have a name. He sure doesn't look like much and he's a little shy, but he's housebroken. He seems so much like he needs a friend."

Slowly, she handed him the dog. He cuddled the forlorn little creature, petting him very gently, since he could see the dog was nervous. He suspected the little dog had been neglected, but Trevor knew that soon this dog would be very spoiled and very happy. Almost hesitantly, the little dog squirmed, his tail made an uncertain wag, and he licked Trevor on the chin.

"I don't know what to say," Trevor choked out as he wiped his chin with his sleeve.

Janice rose on her tiptoes and gave him a peck on the cheek. "Happy anniversary. You ruined my surprise, you know."

He couldn't stop his grin, which he didn't think would leave his face for the rest of the day. He'd wanted a dog for years. They both had. Not long after they were married, they had agreed that they would rescue a dog, and now they had.

"Believe it—you really did surprise me." He gave the dog one more hug, then stepped closer to Janice, trying to figure out some way to embrace her and the dog at the same time. "We've bought a house, and now that we've got a dog, you know what's supposed to happen next, don't you?"

Janice grinned and rested one hand over her stomach. "Uh, Trevor, speaking of surprises. . ."

A Letter To Our Readers

Dear Reader:

In order that we might better contribute to your reading enjoyment, we would appreciate your taking a few minutes to respond to the following questions. We welcome your comments and read each form and letter we receive. When completed, please return to the following:

Rebecca Germany, Fiction Editor
Heartsong Presents
PO Box 719
Uhrichsville, Ohio 44683

1. Did you enjoy reading *The Wedding's On* by Gail Sattler?
   ☐ Very much! I would like to see more books
       by this author!
   ☐ Moderately. I would have enjoyed it more if

   _____

   _____

   _____

2. Are you a member of **Heartsong Presents**? Yes ☐ No ☐
   If no, where did you purchase this book?_____

   _____

3. How would you rate, on a scale from 1 (poor) to 5 (superior), the cover design?_____

4. On a scale from 1 (poor) to 10 (superior), please rate the following elements.

   _____ Heroine   _____ Plot

   _____ Hero   _____ Inspirational theme

   _____ Setting   _____ Secondary characters

5. These characters were special because_____
_____
_____

6. How has this book inspired your life?_____
_____
_____

7. What settings would you like to see covered in future
   Heartsong Presents books?_____
_____
_____

8. What are some inspirational themes you would like to see
   treated in future books?_____
_____
_____

9. Would you be interested in reading other **Heartsong
   Presents** titles?   Yes ❏   No ❏

10. Please check your age range:
    ❏ Under 18   ❏ 18-24   ❏ 25-34
    ❏ 35-45   ❏ 46-55   ❏ Over 55

Name _____

Occupation _____

Address _____

City _____ State _____ Zip _____

Email _____

South Carolina

The female instinct to protect and provide for her family is strong. But can these four Southern women stand up to the challenges that rage against their loved ones?

The ultimate family man is God—but will each of these women turn to Him for counsel? Can they comprehend His lessons on true love?

Contemporary, paperback, 464 pages, 5 ³⁄₁₆" x 8"

❤ ❤ ❤ ❤ ❤ ❤ ❤ ❤ ❤ ❤ ❤ ❤ ❤ ❤ ❤ ❤ ❤

❤ ❤ ❤ ❤ ❤ ❤ ❤ ❤ ❤ ❤ ❤ ❤ ❤ ❤ ❤ ❤ ❤

·····Heart♥ng·····

Any 12 Heartsong Presents titles for only $27.00*

CONTEMPORARY ROMANCE IS CHEAPER BY THE DOZEN!

Buy any assortment of twelve *Heartsong Presents* titles and save 25% off of the already discounted price of $2.95 each!

*plus $2.00 shipping and handling per order and sales tax where applicable

HEARTSONG PRESENTS *TITLES AVAILABLE NOW:*

(If ordering from this page, please remember to include it with the order form.)

Hearts♥ng Presents
Love Stories
Are Rated G!

That's for godly, gratifying, and of course, great! If you love a thrilling love story but don't appreciate the sordidness of some popular paperback romances, **Heartsong Presents** is for you. In fact, **Heartsong Presents** is the *only inspirational romance book club* featuring love stories where Christian faith is the primary ingredient in a marriage relationship.

Sign up today to receive your first set of four never-before-published Christian romances. Send no money now; you will receive a bill with the first shipment. You may cancel at any time without obligation, and if you aren't completely satisfied with any selection, you may return the books for an immediate refund!

Imagine. . .four new romances every four weeks—two historical, two contemporary—with men and women like you who long to meet the one God has chosen as the love of their lives. . .all for the low price of $9.97 postpaid.

To join, simply complete the coupon below and mail to the address provided. **Heartsong Presents** romances are rated G for another reason: They'll arrive *Godspeed!*